Praise for Tyler James Russell

Intense, propulsive, full of dark energy, Tyler Russell's novel envisions the end of the world through the yearnings of two characters barely clinging to what makes them human. Its darkness is irradiated by a sharp wit, psychological depth, and lyricism unusual in a thriller barreling this quickly across the pages. Fans of Palahniuk's *Fight Club*, Flynn's *Gone Girl* or McCarthy's *The Road* will savor these nonstop pyrotechnics.

Robert Rosenberg, author of *This is Not Civilization* and *Isles of the Blind*

A spellbinding thriller about the shattering impact of human trafficking, set in a devastated and dangerous apocalyptic world, Tyler James Russell's brilliant exploration of how the human mind copes with extreme trauma grabbed me on page one and never let me go. Russell's creative language and short riveting chapters kept me glued to the page, desperate to know what would happen, yet I didn't want this remarkable, terrifying story to end. *When Fire Splits the Sky* is the most riveting, original book I've read in ages.

Laura Davis, author of *The Courage to Heal* and *The Burning Light of Two Stars*

This is a welcome reprieve from the simplistic caricatures about someone with multiple personalities that have become common today. No serial killer. No crazy person. Just a look at the alters that fill out the person Ben calls his wife. *When*

Fire Splits the Sky helps us see the humanity and struggles of both Ben and Maranda (et al), as they fight to come to terms with their personal and relational trauma, searching for a path toward mutual healing.

Sam Ruck, author of the blog *Loving My DID Girl(s)*

WHEN FIRE SPLITS THE SKY

A NOVEL

TYLER JAMES RUSSELL

For Cat, of course, with all my love

and E—

and the Peeps

you know who you are

For how do you know, wife, whether you will save your
husband? Or how do you know, husband, whether you will
save your wife?

1 Corinthians 7:16

(I am large, I contain multitudes.)

"Song of Myself," Walt Whitman

PART I

MARANDA

Today's the third time Maranda's called off work to secretly trail her husband, driving up Glacier Highway out of Juneau. She knows it's stupid, but her mind is an in-spiral. What else can you do but follow it?

Ben's been acting different lately. He comes home and paces the kitchen, muttering. She pretends to be asleep on the couch with the TV on, but she's not asleep.

A guy like Ben could've had anyone. He's *ideal.* But he chose her. Maybe, just maybe, that says something about her.

Of course, a voice says, *if he's out here doing what you* think *he's doing, that says something about you too.*

Shut up, she thinks. Shut the fuck up.

For as long as she can remember, Maranda's been accompanied by voices. They orbit her head like moons.

Planets have to hate their moons. No goddamn quiet. Jupiter's got, what, like 70? Probably at least a two-dozen of them are bitches.

The voices talk to her, sure, but a lot of the time they talk to each other too. It's like she's listening to a full room. They've got names, accents. One of them's a dude.

Sometimes, her voices take over. Hip-bump her right out of the frame. Sometimes she's aware of what's going on when they're out, and sometimes she's got no idea it's even happened until she's back. There's no rhyme or reason, really.

She tries not to think about any of this, and sometimes gets long stretches without hearing them. It was worse right after she got out, and then they quieted down for a while when she and Ben got together. But now, now they're going again.

Now she can definitely hear them.

Maranda's a black hole for pain. Pain comes screaming out of the air like jet fighter-knives. They sheathe themselves in her flesh, handles sticking out of her eyes, her chest, her everywhere.

Normal people sometimes feel two things at once. For her it's four, eight, two dozen. Her head is a DVD player that can't read the disk. All the goddamn time.

She checks her phone—twirls it between her thumb and middle finger—but she's not going to call him. If she calls he'll know she suspects.

She tries to swallow the tension in her chest. Something's about to happen.

Haven't you always thought that? a voice says.

Sure, and hasn't she been right?

Her life's a blender. Lid off. The cupboards are spackled with memory and ruin. Chunks of red dripping from her face.

She's always tried to out-drive her thoughts, and the Audi, her car—well, she picked it out—moves like friction isn't a thing. She surges by a minivan that has been going *exactly* 55 for a mile now. As she passes she can feel the mom at the wheel staring at her.

Inside, the dude voice says, *There a problem, bitch?*

Her head is like a daycare. She has to shout to hear herself.

She doesn't have the AC on because she can't stand to have the windows closed. You need to have a little bit of air moving. Otherwise it's a coffin. Plus it lessens the virginal machine-smell Ben tries to hold on to, though she tries not to think about that. Sometimes, if it ever does get hot, she'll drive with the windows down and still let the AC blow. Ben teases her, and truthfully she doesn't feel good about it either, but she still does it. He tells her to imagine all the havoc she's wreaking on poor Mother Earth. The bunnies staggering from foot to foot with one paw to their throats, gasping. She tells him to shut up, and he laughs, and she laughs too. To show that she's in on it.

She turns the radio on. The volume hits like an out-of-nowhere backhand.

"...where summit talks entered the third day. Leaders are committed to..."

She shuts it back off. It feels like she ought to listen to more news stories as an adult and all, but she just can't. At least not now.

She drives another twenty miles. The time blips by like she slept right through it. She's in one place and then another, just like that.

It looks like rain, but spears of glare hit the hood of the car and explode. She takes the exit past Thane, hardly noticing what she's driving through. Everything's at the top of her stomach now. Up against the middle of her chest.

The Audi crunches over gravel. Ben calls this the cabin but it's really a lodge. He's supposed to be out here hunting, but his Land Rover's not in the lot.

Hotels have always been a thing. She hates them. She tells Ben it's because you put your head down where somebody else just did their dreaming but it's so much more than that.

Her whole body's a beehive. Her hands are doing their own thing. She flattens them on her legs as she walks inside, up to the man at the counter.

"I'm looking for my husband, Ben Watters."

"Ben Watters," the guy says. He's wearing a bolo. "Ben. Watters." He clicks through his computer screen. She watches his eyes scroll down, up, down again.

"I'm sorry, ma'am. No one by that name's checked in."

Her life's a blender. Lid off.

Things click into place. In a way, she expected this. At least now she knows where they stand.

Inside she hears the angry voice, the dude, deep and clear, *Well, you knew it, bitch. Didn't I tell you and tell you?*

The dude voice starts taking over. Snakes of fire wiggle in her arms. Fucking electricity, man.

Suddenly she's outside. It's like no time has passed. Like the world moved on without her and now she's entering its course mid-stream.

She's at the car, yanking and slamming the door—over and over and over—without any kind of volition of her own. Her arm keeps at it until someone touches her shoulder, the bolo guy from inside.

"Hey lady, you okay?"

The voice that comes out of her throat is the dude voice, not hers. It's sandpaper. It says, "I look like a fucking lady *to you?*"

BEN

After he and the girl are done, Ben stands in the motel bathroom in his undershirt and boxers, the faucet running water so hot it forms steam-ghosts on the mirror. He's flushed, hair tousled, trying to force himself back into what he considers his true self. This, the guy in the motel, that's not him. Not really.

Ostensibly, he's out here on a hunting trip, but every city, every town, it's always the same thing. It's there if you know what to look for. What else is he supposed to do? How else is he supposed to function, not only in his normal life but also as some kind of support for Maranda? He's supposed to come home and take care of dinner and everything else while she sleeps through the day. The rare times they *do* have sex just lead to fighting anyway. If he didn't have a way to blow off steam he probably would have called it quits months ago.

At least this way—out of town, anonymous—it's not messy. It's biology, a prescription, if you think about it. Maybe a better man would be able to navigate all this without an outlet, but at least now he's able to come back home and be patient with her, without pressuring her to have sex with him when she's clearly got no interest of her own. If anything, she should have some sympathy for him, honestly.

Ben stops. Takes a breath. He's a fucked up guy and he knows it. There's a maw in his belly that swallows each orgasm as soon as it ends. He scoops water over his forearms, pulls out the waistband of his boxers and scrubs himself, then lathes water as hot as he can take it over his chest and neck and face. He grips the edge of the sink, lets his head fall.

He can't do this anymore. He fucking can't.

Driving in, he'd seen in the distance a collection of clouds windblown into the shape of a fist. They were backlit to a bloody orange, edges rimmed with dark. A familiar feeling accompanied it, the kind of brimstone guilt he still associates with his father.

The truth is, he wants to be different. Wants to not be the kind of man who needs sex to shore himself up. All his life he's been limping along, trying to hide it, but all this hiding is about to choke him out. He never comes home feeling anything but dirty, hesitant to touch anything. Like it's not his house anymore. He tries to mask it, tries to make her laugh, but he's a performer in his own life.

There was a couple that came in probably twice a week to the pharmacy where he worked to refill their blood thinners or heart medications, whatever. He can't even remember their names, but a few weeks ago it was just the woman. When Ben realized the old guy had probably passed away, it fell into his head that if he himself died, no one would have known him, like, at all. Since then, he's been feeling the pressing need not only to stop, but to tell her. There's so much she doesn't know. He wants to call, tell her what's been going on, that he wants to stop but doesn't know how, that he's sorry, and that he's certain there's got to be something deep within him, something good—but everything's so grimed over he can't even access it long enough to wrestle it into words.

Through the door, he hears the girl get up and leave. Enough, he thinks, steam rising from his skin. No more.

This was the last time, he tells himself. The absolute last time.

Going out, he nods at the muscular guy in the blazer he paid earlier, but the guy doesn't look up. Thunder rumbles in the distance. Clouds coil. Rainbow smears of oil spread on the pavement.

Ben takes his wedding ring out of his pocket and slides it back on. He tries to will some better part of himself to the fore. And even though the inside of him is all clawed over, he thinks that maybe he can feel something fall away from him as he walks into the evening. Scales from his heart. There's a difference to this day. Like maybe he's on the verge of actually changing.

When he looks up, at first he doesn't recognize the woman with her arms crossed, leaning against his Land Rover's door. Absently, she spins a phone between two fingers.

"Hey," she says, and actually *smiles,* which is scary as hell. Ben freezes, keys still stupidly in his hand, like he might be able to muscle this into a normal or an okay moment.

Maranda raises her eyebrows. "Had a bad feeling," she says. "Were you with someone?"

A pickup pulls into the restaurant next door. It's now or never. Ben tongues the inside of his lip. When he finally speaks there's no volume to it. "Yeah."

For a moment, she doesn't do anything. Like maybe she didn't know what he meant. But then she flinches, blinks hard.

"Mar," he says, but she doesn't hear him. She twists her head to the left like she's cracking it, but he knows she's not. He watches the tremble leave her face as she exhales, closes her eyes, and rolls her neck out again. She turns without saying anything else and marches across the lot.

"Wait," Ben calls, following. "Mar, wait. It's not…Mar!"

She gets in, slamming the door. He stands in front of the car, blocking her, but when he sees her eyes dare-widen, he steps back.

She screeches out. Ben stands with his hands interlocked above his head, squished under some blind malice. A dog barks. He kicks the tire of his Land Rover, then does it again. He doesn't know what the hell he's doing, but before he knows it, he's keyed half the length of a seventy-thousand-dollar SUV. The clouds are breaking into shreds behind him, clots of darkened color bleeding into the clear. He smacks the window again and again, blind and lunatic, like he could raze the thing with his bare hands, wreck it all down to nothing.

The blue-blazered man stares from the window of the motel lobby, scrawling something on the inside cover of his book. He has time to double check it. Then he dials, props the phone against his shoulder. It rings and rings. Holding a lit menthol cigarette, he rubs the corner of a lapel between his fingers, smooths a crease in his jeans. Finally, a woman answers. She tonelessly says his name.

"Just saw the one who got away," he says. "Yeah, definitely her. Price still what it was?"

He is not a man who smiles often. But then he hears his boss's answer.

MARANDA

This time of night their ranch in Juneau holds blue the way a puddle holds water. As Maranda enters the front door the porch-light triangles open, then shuts.

She checks the latch and stands there. Alone. She wants to go to sleep, to not be here and then wake up and have everything that's gone down erase itself. She wants to revert to normal, whatever that is.

But everything's different now. Everything's drained out.

She looks at herself in a mirror. The world operates on cost and worth. Take cars. If the car you're thinking about buying is worth more to you than having the money, you end up buying the car. If the money's worth more, then you don't.

So why wasn't she worth more to Ben?

The dude voice in her head says, *Fuck Ben. Fuck him.*

She was supposed to find a guy, settle in, head south, and her fucked-up past was going to break up like ice. That was the plan, the deal. She held up her end, didn't she?

A voice floats up from the back of her head. Not one of the usual ones. Not Klara or Guardian or Chipmunk or Axel. It's cold, stripped clean. It says: *You know why.*

Maranda thinks, Yeah, I know.

You want a steak, but Hangar on the Wharf is on the other side of town. McDonald's is right here. What's it worth to you? If you stick with the value meal, then it wasn't steak you wanted, was it? You wanted convenience.

Some sun peeks its head over the horizon of her heart. It's huge and hateful. Even as she pulls her mind away, it's still there. Burning.

There's a lot she's never told Ben. For example, the record scratches across her life. About how some days her head makes an evil plastic *skrch* and then the same memories loop over and over. It's a merry-go-round in there, but all the ponies have knives in their skulls.

There are years like a movie she only half-watched. That's when some of the voices took over, she's pretty sure, so it wasn't her out and living then, not literally. Her and not her at the same time. She used to feel like she should tell him more, but now, what does it matter?

The clock reads 9:41. She stares and stares at it.

The walls are festooned with the last year and a half—a collection of their time together. Photographs, concert tickets, origami swans, dried bunches of flowers. Twine is screwed into the drywall and strung in arcs all around the room. Here's a picture of the two of them wearing New Year's glasses. Here's them on the deck of a boat, pink-faced and cold. She doesn't remember who took the picture. Doesn't even remember the boat.

She'd thought he was straight out of a rom-com, but what the hell had she been thinking? A twenty-six-year-old with a good job, endless ambition, an unnecessarily nice car, and no significant exes to speak of. She should have known.

If no one else had been able to stand him, that should have told her something, right?

She's done. She gave it a try, thought a square life would fix her, but who the hell would want this? People are assholes. They'll cut you as soon as screw you. As if she needed any more help believing this.

She feels herself slipping. Soon it's like someone else is moving her body. Her fingers want to rip out of themselves and claw the room to shreds.

Let's trash the goddamn place, Axel growls.

He's a shark swimming the depths of her skin. Wants the walls to bleed.

Just as quickly Axel's gone, and there are photographs all over the floor, twine ripped from the screws. The mirror just inside the doorway holds a dozen shards. On the floor is a shoe she doesn't remember throwing.

How is it after 11:00 already? She's only been home a minute.

She blinks. The world telescopes away. She feels sharper, more precise. Guardian?

Yes, is all the voice answers, and she feels herself move businesslike and calm around the room. She unclips the clothespins and pictures slide to the floor.

A car passes by outside. Light arcs through the blinds. She cracks her neck this way, then that.

She's in the kitchen, no idea why she came out here. She can barely think. If she can just sleep she'll wake up and it will be yesterday again. This will never have happened and she will not know this new thing about Ben, about herself.

Suddenly, it's past midnight. At odds with morning. She's on the couch, carried along by some consciousness-river. The television hums bled-out color. There's a Calico Critter rabbit beside her, and as she moves her hand away from her face she realizes she, a grown-ass woman, has been sleeping with her thumb between her teeth.

She hears one of the voices, a little girl, crying, *Gracie, I miss Gracie.*

Maranda tries to ignore it, like she always does, but fuck, man.

When the doorknob whispers, her mind shoots awake. Ben steps in with his duffel and ghosts the door shut, scans the room to where she has her eyes closed. She feels it happen. Feels him by his noise and weight. She pretends to sleep, composes her face into nothingness.

Part of her feels bad for him. Like, how pathetic do you have to be? But then that gets replaced by numbness, and when he goes past her, toward the bedroom, she opens her eyes and he's no longer her husband. No longer anyone to her. It's so easy, she thinks, for a person to become another person, just like that.

BEN

He eases the door open. The house is blued with television, filled with the laugh-track she keeps herself surrounded by. Now, as always, he's got no clue what he's going to find.

One time he came home and she was sitting on the floor, surrounded by the pieces of a shattered dish. She was running a single shard over the pads of her hands, fingering it, almost lovingly. When he said her name, she jumped. In the other room, the TV was playing menu music on a continuous loop.

He can make out her shape on the couch. She's been sleeping on the couch for a while now, not on the nice one but on the old love seat patterned with *"corduroy"* as she's always called it, a mistake she's always clung to like it's cute or something, and which he's found invariably irritating— because, like, what's adorable about being *wrong*? Russian Roulette's another one; she says it rou-*lay*. Once when they were fighting she said every day with him was like a game of "Russian rou-*lay*."

He told her it was roulette, actually.

"Fuck you," she spat.

He moves as quietly as he can into the kitchen, using his phone's flashlight instead of flipping a switch. Part of him thinks that if he can dodge her for a few weeks it will blow over, but another part of him knows that's stupid. He's committed something irrevocable, not just the cheating but the confessing. His neck's to the stump, now.

Things have been falling apart for a while. Kind of before, but then much more *after* they got married. She started poking holes in his stories. All Ben had was anger. God in heaven, the *fighting*. They'd fight for days without resolution. It would be three in the morning before either of them would let a thing drop, and even then only out of sheer exhaustion, both knowing they would pick it up and set it down again, unchanged, the next day. Last week, in the middle of an argument about who-knows-what, he'd spiked a spoon—a goddamn *spoon*—and now was going to have to pay to fix the divot in the kitchen linoleum. Well, maybe.

Taking a drink, he almost chokes when he turns and finds her not only awake but five feet away. He bends over and coughs into his elbow, then tries to talk and coughs again. He holds up a finger until it passes.

"Hey," he manages.

Maranda tilts her head, watching the floor. She won't look him in the eye. Even given the circumstances he can tell something's off. There's nothing at all on her face that he can read. She kicks one foot at the other in a way that's almost girlish.

He frowns. "Mar? You okay?"

This happens once in a while, and it always brings a lump of fear to his chest that he can't quite swallow. He found out early on there were other people within her, or at least what she called people, rumbling beneath her life like subway cars. Some days the earth holds them down; other days they burst out, no warning. He's only met the one, but where there's one there're always others, right? What worries him is not the personalities, it's what the hell could *do* this to a person?

"Who is this?" he asks, trying to catch her eye.

"I'm not s'posed to say," she whispers, like she's reminding herself.

"Right, okay. Well, I'm not gonna hurt you."

She studies the floor, swallows. "I'm Chipmunk," she says, and looks up at him. The light from the television hits her on the side of the face. He notices she's holding a rabbit. A little figurine in a doll's housedress.

"Chipmunk? Like the animal?"

"Chip-munk."

"Okay, okay. Um, how…how old are you, Chipmunk?"

She makes a face like she's working things out. Bites her lip, holds out one hand and another thumb.

"Six?"

He hears a car, headlights in the front window, blurring across the wall. There are strings of pictures hanging over the backs of the furniture, down onto the floor.

He takes a sip of water. Tries to relax. He wants to direct the conversation somewhere innocuous but before he can she blurts out, "Why'd you do that?"

He opens his mouth and finds himself empty. He sets the glass down. A bubble detaches from the bottom and wiggles upward. He feels her staring at him.

"Maranda's really," she stops. "Why'd you do that?"

He drops his head. He mumbles the word "shit" to himself. "Look, I didn't mean to hurt you. I just…"

"Not me. *Her.*"

Chipmunk closes her eyes. She twists her chin up, to the left. A wince screws up her features. She squeezes her eyes a few times, then opens them.

Dread enters his body like a many-tendrilled fog. He tries to act normal. "I don't know what I'm doing. I'm—"

"Shut up," she says, and by her voice he can tell it's Maranda again. "Just shut up."

She sighs and kneads at the back of her own neck. There's nothing six about her anymore. She's standing differently, every gesture well-lived in. When she opens her hand and notices the Calico Critter rabbit, she tosses it to the couch with disgust.

"Listen," Ben says. "Please, I want to…I'll do whatever you want. Whatever it takes."

She runs a hand through her hair, laughs spitefully. "What does that even *mean*, Ben?"

"I don't know, but I'll…I'll do whatever."

"I really thought I was safe here."

He all but physically feels it. He opens his mouth, but there's nothing to say. In the darkness, in the weak light of the television, her face looks like one he'll never see again.

MARANDA

She's got no memory of the rest of the night. Just—blip, and it's morning.

At the window for the first knife of dawn, what happened yesterday feels like somebody else's dream.

He cheated on her. He cheated on her. She thinks it over and over. Part of her is ready to leave him, but the idea stays outside. Her mind won't make enough room for it.

She'd cobbled a life together. But now—when you drop a glued-together vase, it breaks in all the same places.

Light crosses the living room floor inch by inch.

Then, out of nowhere comes a distant, enormous, concussion. A gong from the center of the Earth.

Everything shakes. A shelf drops from the wall. The picture window shatters inward. The power flicks off, then on, then off again. Ribbons of plaster dust unspool from the ceiling.

Guardian yells: *The archway!* and she falls beneath it, cowering. Ben stumbles from the bedroom, palming the walls.

There's a one-second gap. Things blink away, come back.

She can feel a tremor-remnant in her muscles, like the shockwave has traveled up through her legs and into her interrupted heart. She's sitting on the floor. Her breathing is frantic, arrhythmic. All the outside noises have somehow gotten into the house.

Someone is saying, "Mar, Mar, are you okay?" but they're far off. Like they're talking to somebody else, also named Mar.

She can't think. Something's in the way. There's a hand on her shoulder. She turns, and there's a face, a man's face. She can't place him. He's like a picture that won't come into focus. The power comes back on. Dust continues to shake from the ceiling. The face is Ben, she remembers, her fucking asshole husband who screwed her over.

The television emits a high-pitched wail, the screen a loom of grayscale strings.

Ben exhales, tiptoes to the front window and rips the curtains aside. Little chips of glass clatter. Outside, a fat column of smoke ponders upward from the other side of the mountains. There's a blushing haze above the trees.

"What's happening?" she whispers.

This, this is every day. This is her life. It started inside her, breathing fire, then moved into the world. Catastrophe has leached from her skull.

She feels herself move backward from her own eyes and sees herself as Ben sees her—cowering on the floor, both afraid and ashamed of that fear.

The rest of it happens with her only there by the barest of threads. She woozily tries to stand, but when Ben lurches forward to keep her from falling a tree of vitriol spreads through every vein. He steps away, showing his hands, and she can feel her neck crack, her body move on its own, like a stretching cat. Axel, the dude voice, is getting ready for a fight.

BEN

Maranda's barely there. When Ben touches her arm, she startles and he backs up a step. She shakes her head and looks around the room like she's cataloguing it for the first time.

He can tell right away it's someone else. Even her facial features seem different. She cracks her neck and takes a few steps, circling her shoulders.

"I told her," she says, her voice affected, deep. "I told her about you. But did she listen? Fuck no."

Outside, people are yelling house to house. Sirens. A baby yowls. Involuntarily, Ben glances at his phone. Already, the screen reads NO NETWORK.

"Whatsa matter?" she spits. "Look like you're about to shit your pants."

He pockets his phone, does his best to collect himself. "Who are you?"

"Name's Axel. I'm one of the ones," she pauses, sneering, to tap the side of her head, "in here."

"You're a..."

"A what?"

"You're..."

"A dude? That what you're trying to get out, dickwad?"

Axel feints, and Ben ducks. Axel laughs.

"What's wrong? This too much for you?"

Ben's never seen her like this. This aggressive. She's got to be pretending, right?

She wipes her—*his?*—nose. Walks over to the window.

"Hey, seriously though," Axel says, squinting at the sky. "You ought to get out now. Let her go. She's nuts, right? Crazy stuff. Just go. Better for the both of you."

Ben coughs into his fist. "Mar, come on."

"I'm Axel, not Maranda, motherfucker. I look like a *Maranda* to you?"

"Of course you do. Look, this isn't—you're Maranda."

Axel chuckles, a dry exhalation as he moves to the now-crooked mirror by the front door and ducks to see himself in it. He licks both his hands and starts palm-combing Maranda's hair. "You got a smoke?"

"You don't smoke."

"Again, Maranda doesn't smoke," Axel says, turning away. His hair's half up in a faux pompadour. "*I* do."

Ben feels everything turning. Somewhere, an old tower siren starts. The air tastes chalky. "Can I talk to Maranda?" he asks. His voice sounds far away.

Axel touches his chest. "Are you not enjoying our conversation? Wish I was one of the others?" He juts out a hip and trails a finger up and down his chest, doing what might pass for a Swedish accent. "Wish I was Klara, big boy?"

Ben bites the inside of his cheeks.

"Whatsa matter? Ain't gonna talk now?" Axel moves up so close Ben can smell the morning sourness in his mouth.

"That won't make me go away, you know. Seriously, I know this is too much for you. You should just go. Go."

Ben doesn't say anything. There's a stronger smell in the house now, or maybe Ben's imagining it. Cacophony threatens outside. Doors slamming, people rushing to their cars. Axel's in his face, but Ben knows that in situations like this you only give yourself away by talking. You end up handing over bricks of yourself, one word at a time.

In his periphery, he sees Axel's eyes flutter, reaching a hand to the wall. Thank God, Ben thinks, relief coursing into his gut. It looks, for a second, more like his wife's face again.

"Got ya," Axel says, breaking into a devil-grin. "Still me." He throws back his head, cackling.

Outside, an anaconda of smoke reaches upward. Like the chamber of a long sleeping god has been broken open. A great column of the world, black muscle, crepuscular and intestinal. A car stops in the street, lurches forward, then stops again. A few people are standing with their hands over their heads. Others have bags at their feet. You watch and there are no words.

With the palm of his hand, Axel smacks the wall. "You think shit's hitting the fan out there? It's *nothing* compared to what's going on inside your wife."

The television flickers. It goes to colored lines, and then static blares the room until the ghost of a lone reporter resolves onscreen. Ben frowns. The man is reading from a paper and there are no graphics behind him. When you can finally make out what he's saying the image sputters like it's being rained on.

"…suspect…the bla…Yukon…urging affected…"

The reporter stops to wipe his forehead. He continues but Ben can't hear him. They're not cutting away to anything else. He's not even turning from one camera to another.

"…of Juneau urged to head south…possible secondary…"

The television cuts out again. The room is not a room anymore, it's so filled with outside air. A few cars rush by. Someone is yelling the name "Sam" over and over but Ben can't read the tone. He can't tell if Sam is simply not within earshot, or if the yeller is losing it, or if maybe Sam has been suddenly, miraculously maimed.

MARANDA

A voice comes to her out of the unformed parts. It says her name. She feels rage drip away like ruined sheaves of flesh.

A hand touches her shoulder. She rounds, spooked, and Ben's there.

"What happened?" she whispers. Her head feels smoked with fog.

"You don't *remember*?"

The dream feeling creeps back. She blinks long, shakes her head.

Wait, no. Here's something.

The Earth moving in her teeth. A concussion that knocked breath from her heart.

"I remember the sound," she says. "Huge."

As she says this, the power returns. Energy *thunks* into their TV. You can hear the guy talking before you can see him.

"*...say Anchorage is unaffected, damage to...areas unknown.*"

A picture of Alaska comes into focus. She tilts her head. There's a dot on the map marked *Anchorage.*

A memory-tremor comes rumbling underground. *Anchorage.* The past, as it returns, rattles the rocks and bones underground, her body's own chewy muscle.

She'd shored up a wall in her mind, but she can tell already it has no chance of holding.

Anchorage. What enters her memory is the smell of crayon wax. She sees herself back in the life, a little girl coloring beside her. She left her buddy back there. Gotten herself out but was too scared to look back.

You've been running from this, Guardian says.

Oh god. She has. Running for more than a year. She thought if she ran hard enough this would all drop away but it hasn't. The pressure's only increased. Attached to her is a bungee cord that will, at any second, yank her into the past.

A voice is crying *Gracie.*

Gracie. Oh my god yes. The *one* person she's been good enough for. If she's good enough for Gracie, maybe she's not nothing after all.

There's shit you've got to face, Guardian continues. *It's now or never.*

A door opens in her chest. Light, hope.

Anchorage. She needs to get to Anchorage.

She feels static beneath her fingers. She's a millimeter from the TV. The image has shifted back to the reporter's desk.

"Mar, *Jesus,*" Ben is saying. "What's going on?"

She turns and looks at him. The prideful meanness in his eyes dissolves, but she doesn't answer.

At a time like this, who the hell cares about Ben? What he's done, what he thinks? He's no husband to her. He's smell and animal, the sharp end of a spear. She has to get to

Anchorage. She has to get on the road before things get any worse.

She turns away, leaving Ben open-mouthed, and heads for the kitchen. What do you take? She looks for food, but food's not the main thing, she knows. She needs water.

"What's going on?" Ben says.

"Leave me alone."

"Maranda."

She jerks open the cupboard and a bag of egg noodles crashes to the floor. She ignores them, moves to the next one.

"Maranda."

Seriously, is he deaf? Did he not fucking hear her? "I said leave me alone."

"What are you doing?"

"Where's the water?"

Ben's voice rises. "*What?*"

"Water. It's in bottles. You drink it."

"It's...it's under the sink."

Somewhere she can hear sirens, the sound of people and fear, but they're far off. Ben is panicky, but a beautiful tunnel vision has descended on her. She needs to pack up and get to the car. She's going to Anchorage.

Under the sink she finds a pallet of water bottles. She hefts them up, standing and turning in one motion for the door, but Ben blocks her way.

"Move."

"Just tell me what you're doing."

She goes to step around and he sidles. She's pinned against the counter. Her arms start to shake.

Suddenly, it's like she is watching a movie of her own life, looking out from inside her head. Ben has his arms out.

She's a dragon. Teeth sore for want of something to rip into. Her voice sounds weirdly deep. It's got a serrated edge.

"*Move.*"

Fear goes into Ben's eyes. His eyes drop. And just like that, he obeys.

Then she's back, seated at the forefront of her mind, and everything returns to full volume and color. A siren crescendos and diminishes outside. She sets the bottles beside the door and heads back to the kitchen where Ben is pacing.

"Look," he says. "Can we just *talk* a minute?"

There's no time to talk. No need to. All Ben wants to do is talk but talking doesn't fix anything. You talk long enough with a liar you come up crazy.

"There's nothing we need to talk about," she says, stopping as she sees herself in the mirror. "What the hell is going on with my hair?"

She licks a palm and flattens it, keeping one eye on Ben. When the waters rise up over a man, that's when you need to look out.

"How about Axel?" he finally spits. "Can we talk about *that?*"

"Him," she corrects. "You knew about them."

"By them you mean your *alters*?"

She notes the tone, the way he uses a diagnostic word.

"I knew about one," he says. "Not Axel. Not Chipmunk either, for that matter. Just how goddamn many are there?"

She doesn't answer. When you respond you give away your power, and she just wants to get out of here, get in the car and go.

She turns a circle, ignoring him. Water, food. She's got her phone, clothes. What else does she need? What else?

"It's a he, by the way," Ben says, all casual, as if she hadn't just said exactly this. "You have a person in your head who's a *he*."

She snaps her fingers, plucks a can opener from the drying rack, and drops it in the bag. She grabs the keys from the counter and turns.

"If you can't deal with that, leave," she says. "Sorry they don't all just want to fuck you."

Outside there's enough sirening to shred your brains out. Everything is *now*. The world is thrumming with chaos and the air is pure oxide, but inside her there's no noise. No fuzz. She could hear a bee pissing a mile away.

A pickup roars down the street, mounting the sidewalk and then slamming back into the road. Ben puts his arm out to guard her, and she turns to watch the truck go.

"Oh my God…" Ben whispers, looking up.

To the east, in the way-off distance, the column of smoke ponders upward. Even from here, it might be the biggest thing she's ever seen.

BEN

As Maranda begins to stow things in the Audi, Ben has to force himself to look away from the smoke, but even so he can't fully break its hold on him. It makes him think of the deeper forces of the Earth, the things that propel rock and lava, buckle mountains. Inside, a piece of him falls down.

A grocery bag slips from Maranda's arm. Two cans roll down the driveway. Ben shakes himself the rest of the way present.

"Mar, just tell me where you're going. Please."

Across the street, a woman is carrying a little girl, crying into a phone.

"I'm going to Anchorage," Maranda whispers.

"What? What do you mean?"

The woman fumbles her daughter into a car seat. She's still crying, not saying anything, only crying.

"Why in the hell would you go to Anchorage *now*? You heard the reports. Only…"

Maranda slams the door. She gets right in his face.

"Look," she says. "I don't know if I want to stay married to you, but there's someone in Anchorage I have to see and I'm going."

He can't help it. "A guy?"

"You can stay here, or you can come. I don't care."

He swallows, chews his lip. He glances at the car.

"I'm taking the Audi," she says. She nods at the key scratches all up and down the Land Rover, which he'd kind of forgotten about, honestly.

"Why would you—"

"Because it's *my* car, and because fuck you, that's why."

She looks directly into him until he turns away. He knows it's a pivotal moment, but he can't think. Separating here would be clean, maybe preferable. But he can tell that something is about to happen, both in the world and maybe in him. He could change now, couldn't he? Couldn't he be different?

To the east, the smoke looks like it will never stop rising. Waves of distant heat distort the sky.

Or maybe, he thinks, maybe this is just the way everything dies.

"Give me five minutes," Ben says.

Back inside, he heads for the bedroom, where last night he couldn't bring himself to do anything more than sleep *on* the bed. Was it just last night? What's happened between them seems like another lifetime, years ago.

Outside, he can hear ambulances and fire trucks Dopplering as they pass. He looks around the room. At what has passed for their brief life together.

Their first anniversary was only a month ago, in June. Jesus, had they really only known each other a year and a half? They were practically strangers. He'd fucked her, she'd fucked him, and now they'd fucked each other up permanently.

To be honest, he'd thought they weren't going to be anything more than a hookup, maybe a fling. Maybe that was all it was meant to be. Maybe they'd made too much out of this by getting married, by trying to force it into a shape it was never meant to keep. They got married on a whim, probably some last-ditch effort to salvage things as they started to crumble, the same way moving in together had been. Some people get dogs. Christ—at least they hadn't decided to have a kid.

He grabs a fistful of clothes and stuffs them into the duffel he still has not unpacked.

Now what's he supposed to do? She wants to divorce him, whatever, but is he just supposed to let her head into this mess on her own? What'll happen if she zones out while she's driving? Or if the little one—Chipmunk—comes out again? He's not sure how it all works. Would Chipmunk come out? Can Maranda control that? Does she even know?

He grabs a Browning .22 from a case on the dresser, checks the magazine and refits it. He lays the pistol on top of the clothes and zips the duffel.

He has to go, he knows that. It's probably some BS macho thing. A part of him that thinks he can be her protector, save her from wilderness marauders and she'd fall all over him, forgiving the whole thing. It's ridiculous, sure, but he can't deny it's there.

He's not even sure he wants to be with her at all, but he's not ready to end it, like, *today*. Honestly, this will probably be a twelve-hour thing—like most of her shit—and then she'll stop. Like the time she was going to go back to school, nights or online, but never got past a few Google searches. Still, he knows her well enough to know that if he doesn't at least pretend to go along with her insanity, by the time she gets back the break will be final.

He takes one more look around the room. He's got his phone, clothes, the gun. He hesitates at the shelf beside the bed, where a few of his father's effects are still stashed. When he sees the copy of the New Testament he hasn't been able to either open or get rid of, things tighten in his gut. He pulls it out and holds it like it might bite him.

Inside the cover is a note scratched in thick, angular writing:

BEN, THE RETURN OF THE LORD WILL CONSUME THE UNRIGHTEOUS LIKE FIRE. GUARD YOUR HEART, AND PREPARE FOR HIS RAPTURE.

Ben takes a deep breath. A few hours. A day or two, tops, and then they'll be back and he can look into psychiatric care, or at least marriage counseling or something.

He stands, tucks the book under his arm, just in case. They'll be back. Things will be back to normal soon.

MARANDA

The streets are a clusterfuck, the stoplights all blinking yellow. Either nobody remembers what this means or they just don't care.

They drive past a man standing on his roof, binoculars to his face. There are tire-gouts through his front yard.

She ought to leave Ben on the side of the road and head out on her own. That's her better sense talking. So why can't she listen to it? She's not staying. She's just not deciding yet. There's a difference, she tells herself.

Horns are going everywhere, horns and sirens and engines. People are screaming the way they scream in movies. Beneath decorum you find the real thing. Soon, everything will be driven by hunger. Dangerous time to be a woman.

Deep down, part of her isn't shocked Ben did what he did. She's seen the way the world is, she's looked into the maw most people pretend isn't there. She's looked the dark of the world in the eye as it fucked her, and now she knows what she knows. The thing that pisses her off the most is that he lied. That against her better judgment, he fooled her.

They pull into a Tesoro off 10th. The lights are on, but the store's already locked and chained. As Ben gets out, a cloud of sound enters the car like a swarm of flies.

She keeps her eyes down. You square your eyes to the world and everything looks back.

That's how you get chosen up, the cold voice says. *Without even knowing. That's where restless eyeballing gets you.*

Shut up, she thinks. Just shut the fucking fuck up.

She wants out of the car but there's no place to get out *to*. Wants to bash open her own skull so she can finally breathe.

She spins her phone in her hand, trying to think about its weight, its smoothness, the blurry stars smeared across the cover. But something keeps tickling at the back of her brain.

She knows what it is. Knows exactly what it is.

The past is a dragon. Sometimes she can keep it asleep, but now, in the car, it's waking. She can feel it lumbering, its meaty-ass tail dragging through her stomach. Her muscles are going to whip out, tentacle-like. She imagines pieces of her body bloodflung all over the inside of the car. Pictures the dragon, free and red-glistened, flying heavy as a mountain away from what's left of her.

A truck squeals through the intersection and she backs away from the window. Ducks. For a second, she can't remember where she is, when she is, but someone—something?—is after her.

Calm down, Guardian says inside. *Breathe.*

She tries to think about what's around her, what her senses are picking up, but it's all she can do to string one breath after another. Fragments of the past keep flashing in her mind, the smell of motel sheets, single-use shampoo bottles. She's on her back. A pent-up trick overtop her. The kind that wants it to hurt. She's falling into herself.

The blue-blazered man is driving, finally on the phone, while his younger, unwashed partner is leaning his entire torso out the car's open window. He sits back down and scratches his neck.

"Yeah, the Land Rover was there," the blazered man says. "Nobody home. Her Audi's registered too, but it was gone."

The younger guy, still scratching, takes the handgun from the floor and checks it between his legs. Arms lank with veins. He loads the magazine and sights it out the windshield.

He can hear their boss's voice over the phone. "So you're done?" she says.

"We'll find her," the older man says, and hangs up.

"Dude, everyone's leaving. It's a hogfuck out here."

He turns without a signal onto Main, then catches the onramp back to Egan. Doesn't say anything.

Eventually the young guy shrugs, sets to scratching his neck again.

"You better not have fleas," the driver says.

"Fuck you." There's a Dodge ahead of them, two coolers bungeed into the bed. He takes aim, fires a mime-shot.

BEN

As the tank fills, Ben pops the trunk to check their supplies. Cans of food, water, a few blankets. Enough for a week, probably, though he's hoping they'll be back tomorrow.

Cars are lining up in the street. Somebody yells for them to hurry the hell up.

He'd had the presence of mind to grab three gas cans from the garage. As he elbows the trunk shut he drops the one and shunts it into the lot where a truck growls just past his fingertips, close enough that warm exhaust briefly envelops him. The dented can goes spinning across the macadam. The truck continues over the curb and onto 10th.

"Fucker," Ben mumbles.

The Audi's tank is already topped off. He holds the plastic cans one at a time and sets to filling them, shimmery fumes leaking from the neck. Caps the second one and is started on the third when he glances into the car and the bottom falls out of his stomach.

It's empty. Maranda's gone.

He smells gas and looks down. There's a slapping warmth around his feet. It takes him a second of staring stupidly at the overfill before he thinks to un-trigger the pump.

Glass shatters nearby. There's a hole in the convenience store's window, and the rest of it is spidered white. Maranda lifts a propane tank by the collar and lobs it in a wide, one-handed arc. Then she kicks out the lower shards before ducking into the store.

That's one way.

He keeps looking over his shoulder at the window as he finishes the cans. Her hair had been pompadoured again, which apparently means it was Axel?

"Good," he says. "That's great."

He finishes and replaces the last can in the trunk of the car. Axel marches across the lot, smacking a pack of Marlboro's against his palm, an unlit one between his teeth.

"What?" Axel holds his hands out like, *you got a problem?*

"Finished?"

Axel laughs. "Now I am. Let me drive."

"No," Ben says, quickly. "No. Come on."

Traffic is hell. He tries to head north but Egan is blockaded, so he turns onto 10th instead. A police cruiser rushes by.

In the passenger seat, Axel cups his hands around a cigarette. Ben's not a smoker anymore but he'd kill for one now, for the weighted blanket it lays over your nerves.

"Let me bum one?"

Axel grips the cigarette between thumb and forefinger, takes a long drag, exhaling toward the roof. "Fuck you."

"We really should be in the Land Rover."

"Mm."

"So why aren't we?"

"Maybe cause she doesn't know what you *did* in that car, Benny. So, no."

Ben coughs. There's a lot he's not thinking of, apparently.

There's a fire engine in the rearview mirror, lightbar blaring. Ben tries to get a little further, but the driver starts laying on the horn. He jerks the Audi out of the way. The asshole passes them so close you can feel the car rock away and then back.

Axel smacks the dash. "Here! Turn here!"

They corner over the curb. A minivan skids out of their way.

"One way street," Ben growls.

"Hey, you wanted to drive. This is shorter. Left. Take McAllister, then get 12th back to Glacier."

Ben's not sure how smart is it to take directions from *whatever* Axel is, but he's got no better ideas. He swerves onto McAllister, but it's backed up all the way.

Ben leans out the window, trying to see around. Far ahead, two police cruisers are parked nose to nose, and next to them is a black dude in a rain slicker and tie with a white signboard that says *Trust in Jesus.* He's making eye contact with Ben. Sound drops away. Traffic presses behind them.

Axel's voice comes in. "Get back on 11th going east. You can catch it that way."

The world returns to full volume. "I know," Ben barks. "*I know.*"

Axel sits back, hands up. "Not out to see whose is bigger, man."

Ben wrestles the car around, wincing as it screeches against a pole. He wishes, again, they were in the Land Rover.

"But mine is, for the record," Axel mumbles.

As they drive the other way, Ben can't *not* check the mirror. The guy's still watching them. Behind him, the line of smoke has only grown. The mountains are smeared with flame.

When they pass a silver Audi going the wrong way, the blazered guy brakes hard, and his partner lurches into the dash.

"The fuck?"

"That was her," he says, U-turning over the strip.

A Jeep rips around them. A few cars up it catches a fire hydrant and flips into the opposite lane, spinning halfway around on its hood. One car swerves to miss it but the next hits just right and the thing spins like it was made to do so. He veers over the rumble strip, braking. He tries to back up, but a truck is already holding them in.

He takes out his phone, dials a number. He holds it away from his face and glares at it and puts it back against his ear.

"They're going North. North. I don't know. We're following." He hangs up.

He slips the Pilot into neutral and roars the engine. He flips off the truck behind them and revs the engine again and the truck backs up a few feet, enough to let them turn.

"Why's there so much money on this bitch again?" the scratchy guy asks.

"Only girl she ever lost."

"No shit?"

"No shit. You want a bitch like that out there talking?"

His partner sits back, nodding. Opposing traffic goes by in a blur.

BEN

When they pull into the Juneau Terminal of the Marine Highway there are four ships waiting in the harbor, small against the mountains, and two men in orange vests trying to funnel traffic while looking over their shoulders at the smudges of sky-fire.

Ben parks with a jolt. Maranda's still Axel, still not his wife. She stubs out one cigarette in the ashtray only to immediately light another. Ben's got no idea how to handle this. What to say. What he wants to do is ignore it and wait for her to come back, or whatever he's supposed to call it.

The lot is emptying fast. Baggage sits unclaimed along the curb, on benches. There's a trampled newspaper on the sidewalk, a single page flapping like the wing of a dead bird. A flag rattles and bangs against its pole.

"Wait here," Ben says.

"Sure thing, boss."

Ben gets out before he can say anything stupid. Is this how the whole thing's going to be? It doesn't matter that he's going along with her insanity, no, she's going to twist his failure in him for all it's worth. He has the brief impulse to leave the car and run, just sprint down the side of the highway. Who would blame him? He could run away and all of this would be left behind.

There's a noise in the sky. He looks up in time to see a flaming jetliner describe a forty-five degree angle toward the earth, then disappear beyond the mountains.

At the end of the dock, a stream of passengers jostle and curse their way down the ramp. A man in a white captain's hat and one arm in a jacket pushes his way through the crowd and heads for the parking lot. Ben follows.

"Excuse me," he calls. "Hey, sir!"

The captain glances back but keeps running.

"Hey!"

The guy goes for a blue Corolla, patting his pockets for the keys. As he starts unlocking the door Ben smacks his hand out of the way.

"Hey, screw you man," the captain spits.

"I need on the next northbound ferry."

"You cracked?" He starts for the door again. Won't even look Ben in the eye. Ben grabs him by the shirt. For a quick moment you can see the glimmer of a question come into the guy's face, is he about to get hit? Ben's got no plans to, but it makes him happy the guy's wondering.

"Come on," Ben says. "It's my wife."

The captain straightens his jacket. "Go to hell man. Get south while you can. Or home. Nobody's going that way."

He pushes Ben two-handed, and then is already in his car with the door locked before Ben can do anything. Ben runs alongside, pounding on the roof, until the guy floors it, fishtailing rubbersmoke onto the highway.

"Shit," Ben mumbles. There's nothing to punch. The world's gone weird and orange. In the air is the sound of blare and clangor, the rattle of traffic, but it's far off. Here everything's quiet. Even the two men directing traffic have fled. Ben feels again, sharply, the cusp on which everything is tottering. It's going to fall. He's all but certain it's going to completely and spectacularly collapse.

He glances at the Audi but can't bring himself to go back to her yet. Once he goes back it's over. This was his only chance.

Instead he walks the other way, further onto the dock. At the end is a flatbed ferry that's little more than a miniature skiff with an American flag on the bow. At first he doesn't notice the guy doing his rounds like nothing's the matter. He's small, a little old, dressed in casuals and a white pork pie. Ben coughs to get his attention.

The man glances up but goes immediately back to his checks. "All passengers supposed to disembark. Get one of the others going south."

"I need to get north."

The man takes his hat off and wipes his forehead. He squints at Ben. "I'm sorry."

Beyond the mountains, it looks like something has punched through the Earth's crust and is drawing its innards out hand over hand.

"Please," Ben says. "It's…"

"Look. I'm sorry."

The captain goes back to his checks. The ferry moves gently against the dock. Ben opens his mouth but there's nothing more to say.

MARANDA

Suddenly, she's in the car again.

What the hell? She was just—

Wait, where *was* she?

She remembers the driveway. No, the gas station. She must have fallen asleep. But she doesn't remember falling asleep. It's late afternoon, by the looks of it, but she's tired. Man, she's tired.

There's a taste in her mouth ungodly strong. She looks down to find a cigarette in her left hand. The hell? She jabs the half-smoked thing into the ashtray.

Axel, she thinks, and hears, *Yo.*

Everything is going more and more strange.

Ben's standing at the far end of the parking lot, turning in a circle with his fingers in his hair. She feels Axel laughing at him.

Guy dresses like a tool, Axel says. *Like a guy in a Woolrich catalogue. And hey, Mar, while I'm at it, why don't you have a leather jacket? Metal studs or whatever. At least different pants. There's no room for a dick in these jeans.*

She shakes her head, tries to clear it out. Axel chuckles.

What's Ben doing out there? Maybe he's leaving, she thinks, but she doesn't get out of the car. She won't chase him. If he leaves, he leaves.

Plus, if he leaves, maybe she can actually drive by herself. He won't even let her open the door right now. She's not helpless. And *manners* sure as hell aren't going to fix things.

Still though, it nibbles at her. Good old insecurity. *Is* he going to leave her? Is she not enough to even *try*?

She hunches her shoulders up and buries her hands in her pockets, where she feels the toy rabbit. She doesn't need to take it out, just rubs its head a little. She thinks about Gracie and joy—weirdly strong—bubbles up inside her.

She jumps when the door opens.

Ben's hesitating at the door, like he's been waiting for her to see him. She blinks. God, was she asleep again?

"Hey," he says. "Is this…?"

"It's me."

"Okay," Ben nods, head down. It's like he's working himself up to re-enter the car. Is he actually afraid? Of her? Ever since last night, he's acted like there are a thousand invisible trip wires attached to her body.

Good, she thinks. There are.

Let the dickwad dance, Axel says. *Deserves to piss his pants a little.*

Finally, Ben gets in and closes the door. He takes a long breath, but she already knows what he's going to say.

"Look," he starts. "We can't…"

"I know."

It was supposed to be simple. All she wanted was to be good enough for someone, at least for Gracie. They hadn't been turning her out when Maranda got away, but her ex, Luke, was a Gorilla, and Louise was all business. They'd start seasoning her soon—there were always people waiting on the kiddie track.

For once in her life things had been beautifully straightforward. She was going to do something good, now this. Every day you turn out your pockets and the universe reminds you of bills you can't pay.

All this goes through her mind in a blink-flash. Out in the water, waves cover and then recede from the pylons. Another car pulls into the lot. Ben leans up and touches the rearview mirror, tilting it down to eye-level.

"What now?" she asks, when there's a flat *bang* off the trunk.

Time turns to sludge. The whole car hums.

Bullet, Guardian yells. *That was a bullet,* but her mind won't turn over. It won't accept this cold fact as real.

Things are happening at a remove now. She looks at Ben. Everything is slow. His hand is still on the mirror. Mouth open, dumb. All of this in the fraction of a fraction of a second. Then the corner of the rear windshield bursts inward, and it's like someone grabs her mind by the collar and yanks her away.

She watches the rest from inside. Sees her every movement go sharp. Even her thoughts, weirdly, aren't panicked.

They're orderly and clean, which is how she realizes she's watching somebody else—Guardian, it feels like—take over.

There are pebbles of glass in her scalp. Guardian unfastens the seatbelt and ducks. Another gunshot. Ben stomps the accelerator, and the car galumphs over a parking block and squeals onto the ferry.

"Ben, get me the gun," she hears herself order. Ben throws it in park, reaches back, but two bullets punch the door and he stops.

She can hear the captain somewhere nearby. His voice is at a fever-pitch. "Hey! What the hell is this?" he's screaming. A bullet ricochets.

"Ben, the gun."

Ben finally gets the handgun, but instead of handing it over, he just points it awkwardly out the open door, not aiming. He doesn't even shoot. Sparks fly from the deck maybe twenty feet away. She feels the ferry sputter and move, the gunfire a random storm about them. Soon there's thirty feet between them and the dock, fifty. One more gunshot. Then nothing.

She watches Ben out of Guardian's eyes. He looks pathetic, breathing like something caged.

He froze, Guardian sighs. *Ben completely froze. And he goddamn knows it.*

BEN

After a few minutes, Ben makes his way to the navigational cabin, still shaky. His reflection's waiting for him in the glass of a vending machine. A dark Ben-shadow.

He'd completely chickened out. When it was time to shoot, he couldn't do it.

Jesus, he'd felt like a kid again. Like he was eight years old in the woods back in Tennessee, sighting the deer with his father over his shoulder and he couldn't do it, couldn't pull the trigger. His father shaking his head, wiping his mouth.

Ben is digging for change in his pocket when the captain enters.

The lights come on. The captain sniffs. "Care to explain why people are shooting at you?"

Ben puts another quarter into the machine. The nozzle coughs, starts spitting something that's supposed to be coffee.

"I'm not out here to get killed," the captain says. "Orders are to go south, not north."

Ben sighs, turning around. The captain's just a guy, just another person probably dealing with his own garbage too. And honestly Ben doesn't want to be doing this either.

He takes a few bills and stuffs them in the guy's shirt pocket. "I don't want any trouble," Ben says.

The captain lifts an eyebrow. He takes the money out and leafs through it. "As soon as you're over there, I'm gone. There probably won't be anyone to get you back."

Ben nods. "Just get us across and I'll double it."

The captain folds the money and stuffs it away. "What's north anyway? Why? With..." He opens his hands, meaning—*everything*.

Ben takes a long breath. He tries, but he's got no idea how to answer that.

It's almost dark. The Gastineau is wide and lonesome. Ben maneuvers both coffee cups into one hand and gets his phone out to check the time. As soon as he glances at the screen he remembers exactly where in the bedroom he left his charger.

Shit.

Twenty one percent. He groans, putting it away. There's nothing to do about it now. He just hopes they won't need it. And that he won't have to tell Maranda.

She's standing at the prow, wrapped in a blanket. At least he thinks it's Maranda, from the way she's standing. She looks glass-thin. Like the smallest thing will shatter her.

A cold wind presses at his face. The sky is starless, and there's smoke beyond the mountains, flickering with the light of an unseen fire.

All he's hoping for is to stay alongside her on the way to Anchorage, even if it's just to drive out a few hours and turn around. Already, this plan has smoothed out the wrinkles in his mind, given him purpose. He could help her, couldn't he? Is that too much to think?

He goes gently across the deck, holding one coffee cup between his thumb and index finger and balancing the other on the palm of the same hand. When he touches the small of her back she recoils.

"Sorry," he says. "Just me."

Wordlessly, he offers the coffee. Wordlessly, she declines. She leans on the railing and looks over the water. The sky is auroric.

"What *was* that?" Ben says. "Who the hell would shoot at us?"

She doesn't say anything. Probably some crazy person, he thinks. What *won't* people do in a catastrophe? There's no reason anyone would be following them. Right? Ben always paid, never got mixed up in the wrong kind of place, but even as he thinks this he starts to worry. If it's used to eating, guilt will follow you even when there's nothing in your pockets.

Mostly he's trying to make conversation. Chipmunk, Axel, he's got a sense *another one* was out during the shooting, which terrifies him—but the way she doesn't say anything for so long makes him wonder if she *does* know, and that's even worse.

Finally, she shrugs. "Maybe they thought we were somebody else."

"Yeah," he says. "Maybe."

She stands up and looks him dead in the face. There's a stray hair by her temple, longer than the others and dancing in the wind. "It's a family member," she says. "In Anchorage. Not a guy."

Ben twists his mouth. He looks down, studying the contours of the coffee lid. "Who?" he asks.

"I'm not—I'm not ready to talk about that yet."

Ben kneels and puts one coffee down. He stands holding the other.

"Just because you're going with me…" she starts.

"I'm only trying to help."

"Yeah, well, you've done plenty already."

He stops, the cup half raised to his mouth, biting the inside of his cheek. He doesn't break eye contact until she turns back to the prow and hides herself more deeply in the blanket.

"I don't need another person fucking with me," she mutters.

Ben takes a sip of his coffee. They cross water that looks to be on fire.

PART II

BEN

They'd had fun once, hadn't they? He can hardly remember it now—even though it's only been, what, a year and a half?—but she used to smile when he walked into a room. Often enough it felt like one big laugh, which helped make up for the times it wasn't. Like when she suddenly had no interest in sex anymore, or when she said—out of the blue— that she probably wouldn't live much longer.

Or when she set out to Anchorage in the middle of a goddamn disaster, driving a fucking luxury sedan, and wouldn't even tell him why.

They'd met at his company's Christmas party, in a pseudo-swank banquet hall where she worked part-time. She made good money, actually, with the semi-performative talents she seemed unendingly capable of. They didn't use drink trays, but she could carry four glasses in one hand— one between her thumb and forefinger, another across her middle and ring, a third in the palm, and a fourth stacked on top. It looked effortless, like everything else she did. She could usually take seven tables before she even had to rush— whereas the other girls topped out at four.

For the record, *she* approached *him*. Just sat down with a burger, still on the clock, still in uniform, and started eating.

"Fuck," she moaned.

When Ben raised his eyebrows and laughed, she covered her mouth. "Sorry," she said. "Hungry."

They hadn't talked after that, but at one point in the evening she walked past him and trailed three fingers across his back. A totally unnecessary thing. For the rest of the night he couldn't think about anything else.

On the other side of the channel, it's another world.

"Jesus," Ben whispers.

There's a swath of felled trees as far as you can see, like an enormous machine dragged over and pressed them flat. On either side, the ones still standing are either actively smoking or glowing with ember-veins. The air is choked, the mountains scabrous and raw. Far off, the fire sounds like something chewing.

Maranda insists on driving awhile. Neither of them speaks. Ben has his hands in his lap, staring straight ahead. He pulls his phone out and checks it. He has the urge to call the pharmacy, to let them know he won't be back until tomorrow, probably, but the signal's periodically unreliable and the battery's already dwindled to 15%. It's insane anyway, of course nobody's there, but being stretched this far from the normal-everyday makes him feel dried-out and snappable. He shuts the phone off, puts it away.

On the ferry, he'd covered the rear windshield with duct tape and a flannel blanket. Crudely done, but it keeps the air out, flapping noisily as they drive. Every so often you can hear the glass strain.

Otherwise, the car is filled with an unnatural quiet. There's nothing to do but talk, Ben thinks, but if they start talking there's really only one way the conversation can go—

other than, you know, the fucking world being on fire—and that's toward him cheating. He'd like to skirt the edge for as long as he can, at least until the bleeding's stopped, and maybe eventually she'd realize it's best to just throw dirt over the whole thing and pretend it never happened. Let the past be the past and they can move on.

After a while though, not talking starts to feel loud. He worries that if he doesn't at least *try*, she'll feel victimized by that too.

A Chevy with a beat up cartop carrier passes them going the opposite way. Ben twists in his seat to watch it evaporate into the haze. A minute later two other cars approach side-by-side, and Maranda has to slow until they merge and pass.

He clears his throat, thinking it a small act of courage, but before he can even get out a word Maranda punches the radio on, filling the car with snowy noise and blare.

Ben sinks back. You work up your courage and that too isn't enough.

She twists the dial, and the sound shifts, like wind is blowing through the static. Soon it clears to a man's voice, flat, unaffected.

"...cause is still unknown. Forest fires...sweeping westward, and east toward the Northwest Territories...in many places..."

There are the accompanying sound-effects of a news bulletin, which Ben finds a small comfort. The normalcy of it. It emboldens him enough to reach up and turn the radio off.

"What?" Maranda says. "What are you doing?"

"I want to talk. About Axel, the others. All of this." Ben leans against the door, facing her.

"Well, I don't. That's why I turned the radio on."

"Hey, c'mon."

"That's right. That's right." She nods, pantomiming already. "I forgot. We talk when you want to talk. You fuck when—*who*—you wanna fuck."

"You always say we ought to talk. Get it out there."

She's not even listening, just going on with her act. "That's right. I forgot how this relationship works."

"So let's just get it out there."

"Nothing matters except *you,* I forgot."

"Listen!" His voice goes louder than he intends.

Maranda blinks long.

Taking a breath, Ben gets a fist around his anger and tries to muscle it back down. "I think I deserve to know who's living in my wife. Do *you* even know?"

Her head twitches once, twice, to the left. The car drifts slightly, vibrating as the tires hit the rumble strips.

"Great," Ben mumbles. He reaches over for the wheel.

For a second it seems like she's actually sleeping. Her eyes are closed and her hands are offering no resistance whatsoever. He bites his lips, too momentarily furious to be afraid. How the hell is he supposed to manage this? How can she be this goddamn helpless? But then, even as this is going through his head, she cracks her neck and opens her eyes, immediately, fully present. She glances at his hands until he takes the hint and sits back.

Her lips are pursed to a tight line. Her posture's so straight it's almost unnatural.

"Relax," she says, flatly. "I'm not Axel."

It's only when she says "relax" that Ben realizes his hands are shaking. Each switch is like standing in front of a door with no idea of what's going to come out. Inside, every time, he wants to hide.

"You can call me Guardian."

"Guardian?"

"Mm. Check the glove compartment, please," Guardian says.

Ben hesitates. He imagines opening to a gun Guardian will snatch and train on him, but all that's inside is a vinyl insurance book, an old map, and a glasses case. Guardian takes the case and polishes the lenses on a shirtsleeve before donning them.

"I didn't even know she *had* glasses," Ben says.

"Neither does she."

The glasses are thin and frameless, could be men's or women's. The same as Guardian, but Ben doesn't know how to ask that. He's pretty sure, at least by the voice—restrained, buttoned up—that this was the same person who was out during what he's now thinking of as the mix-up at the ferry.

"Guardian," Ben says. "Like an angel?"

"No."

Ben opens his mouth, closes it, nods. He unfolds a panel of the map and pretends to study it. It's a lucky find, with his phone and all, but all it shows is a mostly blank green anyway. A few squiggled roads here and there.

"You're from Tennessee," Guardian says.

"Kingsport."

"So you're just as green out here as we are. Maranda's been around but…well."

Most likely he—she?—means "been around" as in travelling, but still. It's a loaded phrase. Ben folds the map back up.

"What's in Anchorage?" Ben ventures. "What, uh, what *happened* to her?"

"That's for her to tell."

"Isn't she, you know, you?"

Guardian sighs, lifting a hand from the wheel and drawing a halo-like circle around Maranda's head. "Do you want to know how this works, Ben? The whole thing?"

He's still kind of irritated about the business with the radio, honestly, and with how goddamned complicated everything is, with how he can't just be a guy with a normal relationship, but he tries to swallow that as best he can.

"Sure," he says.

On a nearby mountain, the world burns. A veil of smoke holds clouds to earth, and every so often an arc of flame plashes upward. Ben watches that instead of trying to maintain eye contact with Guardian.

"During repeated instances of trauma, usually sexual…" Guardian glances at Ben. "You knew."

"Some. She doesn't like to talk about being a kid."

"During repeated instances of trauma, a person's psyche starts to fragment. Into pieces. At least, Maranda's did. It's too much, literally, for one person. So her mind made others—us—to share the load."

"So, like, after. After, one of you…"

"An alter."

"After, an alter would form?"

"Sometimes. Sometimes during. Sometimes one of us went through it so Maranda didn't have to."

"Jesus. I knew about…I've met Klara before."

"More than met."

"She doesn't…doesn't seem to mind."

Guardian shrugs. "No. She's a sufferer, though. Don't let her fool you. It's easier to like sex than fight it. And now Axel. You've met Axel too."

"And Chipmunk. But you seem different."

Ben expects a smile, a flattered ego, but Guardian emits nothing.

"I'm the gatekeeper. You can ask to talk to any of us, request someone, but I have the final say. Who gets to go out, when, what situation."

"You're the C.O."

Guardian makes a face, like the title doesn't quite fit. "We all have different roles."

"So, what, like Axel comes out when she's stressed? Klara for sex?"

"It's more complicated than that. I try to make sure the person coming out is suited to deal with the situation. There have been a few *messed up* situations at hand. Sometimes they just need some time out, in the light. Sometimes the person coming out may seem anomalous but they're the right one, the perfect one, for the job, so to speak. I'm good at what I do. There's a rhyme and a reason. But from the outside, it doesn't always look like that."

"She's not normally like this. All the switching, I mean."

"No."

"But now it's, like, constant?"

"Are you asking why, or if it's real?"

Ben thinks a moment. "I think I'm asking why."

Guardian nods. "Look outside."

Ben does, sees a whip of fire tendril up and disappear, leaving an after-image of smoke. "Okay."

"We help Maranda cope with chaos and trauma. And right now, being in this car with you is just as much a threat as anything outside."

Ben doesn't voice any of what first bubbles into his head. Instead, he keeps his voice low. "She's…it seems like she's barely hanging on."

Guardian shrugs. "*We're* hanging on fine. She's not incompetent, Ben."

"I know that."

"Do you?"

Ben sighs. "How many of you are there?"

Guardian doesn't say anything, not even a shrug.

"More?"

For a single, panicked moment, Ben sees his wife as an infinite regression, one within the other, like smaller and smaller matryoshkas. He wants, instinctively, to know how many there are, and which ones are actually her.

"It's crazy," Ben says.

"No," Guardian's voice is immediate, sharp. "It's not."

"I'm just…"

"It's not crazy. It's the opposite of that. It's what kept her *not* crazy."

All of a sudden, a memory goes through Ben's head. A time they'd been arguing, and later that night Ben leaned in and tried to kiss her, tried to maybe start something.

"You're joking," she said, pulling back.

"Come on."

He moved in again, a little pushy this time, and she froze. She didn't move or speak or even blink. After a minute of this he backed up to his side of the bed and she flinched, shook her head, and glared like she could bore holes through him.

That probably wasn't Maranda at all, was it? When she finally "came back" she was as docile as ever, just rolled over and went to sleep. They never talked about it afterward.

Ben watches Guardian's face and clears his throat. "Yeah, I just mean, it's…it's complicated. It's tough."

"Look," Guardian says, hands opening and closing. The leather makes a flexing, releasing sound. "However tough *you* think this is, we're the ones who went through it."

Ben holds eye contact with Guardian until he can't anymore. Outside, the blasted trees are a mutable blur beyond the glass.

MARANDA

For years Maranda never got back to the house until the first burn of dawn, so all she saw of a given day was the end and beginning of it. She'd come back and shower until someone started banging on the door, or until the water went cold, but you could never wash enough.

One of the bad nights, the kind she only remembered fragments of, she got back and laid down, one ear ringing, her toes and ankles twice-blistered. As soon as she closed her eyes Gracie was on the bed. She hadn't even heard the door open.

"Can I sleep with you?" Gracie whispered, her voice close, insect-small.

As they drive, her mind goes all over. It's a goddamn bird. She can't get it to land—to *stay*—anywhere.

That's just one of the things wrong with her.

She's rotten. Deeply rotten. If you'd cut her open, there'd be black spots, like in a potato. Probably smell, too.

There are almost no memories in her head before age six. She can sometimes fool herself into thinking it works that way for everyone, but if she ever thinks too long about that before-six blackness, some hidden beast starts growling.

What she does know of her early years comes second-hand from her father. That her parents lived a spell in Arizona, some commune-thing, a dozen trailers in the middle of the desert waiting for, whatever, a comet or something. That's where Maranda's mom got pregnant. A year later, when she went east with some guy she was blowing on the side, her dad headed north with this kid who was maybe not even his kid. He made sure she knew that.

Maranda ran away from him when she was fourteen, and everything around that is a dropped plate. Now and then a memory seeps through, blood through a bandage. A coffee table, a beige carpet. A doctor shining a flashlight into her eyes, asking about a fall she doesn't remember taking. It's just the shore, she knows. Beyond that is so much sea.

Now she's heading for Anchorage, diving headfirst into the past. She's got to be batshit.

She sits in the passenger seat and tries to say as little as possible, allowing herself to be driven. She spins her phone around and checks it, but it won't make calls. Nothing works when you want it to.

They make their way into what she always assumed was the wild. She's surprised to find as many houses as they do, but now they're all half collapsed. Gables pulled sideways, roofs caved in, rooms exposed to hell-sky. Everything delicate is gone. In the east, constantly, is the column of smoke or vapor. It unspools like a vertical river, up and up and up.

The world has never seemed so frail, so on its way dead.

Maybe she'll be wiped into nonexistence. Like the way the sky used to be and may never be again. Like the color green. She thinks about all the ways she could die. Plays it on a continuous loop in her brain. She might be walking and trip. The pavement coming up closer and closer until a common, flat-bottomed nail goes right into her skull, and the yolk of her brain leaks out, hissing and bubbling. She rewinds, slows it down. This time she twists and it goes in the side, under her hairline. Same result. Again and again and again. It takes no effort on her part to imagine this. This is where water flows most naturally through her mind.

She's made a mistake, coming out here with Ben. She ought to be alone. Nobody can hurt you if there's nobody around.

She'd always intended to go back for Gracie, but she couldn't face it. If they caught her they would kill her too, and who would that help?

No, that's not it. She should have done this a long time ago. She was plain old too afraid. It's only now—now that *everything* in her life is on fire—that she's got nothing to lose.

There have been so many things Maranda didn't want to see. With Ben, with Gracie. If she saw any of them she'd have to acknowledge that her husband only cared about his dick, or that Louise was prepping Gracie to be just another one on the track. Like how Ben insisted on showering as soon as he got home, or the time Gracie came in cradling her wrist, and there on the back of her forearm was a perfect cigarette circle. Maranda had held her, let her cry, but she didn't ask, and Gracie didn't tell.

All around them, the world burns. Maranda feels almost nothing about it. It barely registers. The world has always been on fire, ever since she was little.

The sky bleeds. Flame in the rock.

She has to find Gracie. That's all that matters. If she can find Gracie she can make at least one thing right.

Eventually Ben slows the car to a stop. He gets out, leaving his door open, and stands with one elbow on the roof. Maranda gets out too.

Before them is a river. There are concrete pylons still standing on either side, but the bridge is completely washed out, and the road cants down into the gray water where chunks of concrete and asphalt have blocked most of the water. Everything's scorched. On the other side, the pavement is fissured and buckled.

The few pines left standing are burnt to skeletons. There's one all by itself, still disgorging smoke, which looks like a man on fire.

In the middle distance she can see the tail of a jetliner sticking out of the trees. She is glad—incredibly, almost blindly thankful—not to be able to see it any closer. There's nothing living anywhere. Maybe she and Ben both are already dead, sucked down along with everything else. For a moment, she's all but certain that's the case.

She looks over the top of the car, wondering if Ben is feeling any of this too, but he's already getting back in and closing the door.

They find a service road going parallel to the river. Farther down, Ben's able to nudge through a thin spot in the trees, out onto the riverbank.

There's little left of the water but an oblong reflection in the middle. The rest is mud and trash, fragments of metal built up with rust. She can feel a tension emanating from Ben. He's holding his breath. She starts to ask, "What are you…?" as the car starts to inch forward, out into the mud.

"I'm not any happier about it," he mumbles, and lurches down over the edge of the road, onto the river bottom. The tires instantly slip. You can hear the cam whining.

She looks downriver, where water leaks from beyond chunks of concrete the size of busses. Water foams through the cracks.

She feels herself get fuzzy. Thoughts intrude.

She pictures, perfectly, the house where she lived as a girl. A double-wide, palo verde in the front. Home.

Immediately, the voices in her head start arguing.

No, don't call it home.

What else would you call it?

Anything. The house where you lived. There.

She has vague impressions of her father leaving her with men or bringing them here. Afterward he'd buy her something or take her out to eat. They never had money, so it's not hard to draw the connections.

Now it's the middle of the day and she's alone with him. He's watching something on the TV and he doesn't see her.

But her mind won't go any further. A wall stops it right there.

Maranda shakes her head. She's back in the Audi, in the present, but her insides are suddenly coursed with fire. What the hell? There's a pain behind her belly button that digs all the way through muscle, down into her thighs.

She bites her lip and turns to the window, clenching her belly against the burn.

They're hardly any farther into the river, only a few seconds, maybe, but it feels like she was gone much, much longer.

Ben drives them up and over a spine of river rock, and she can feel it scrape all down the bottom. Ben winces.

Inside, a voice is saying: *He's going to bust the suspension.*

Axel, she thinks. Maranda says something, but it feels more like her saying it *for* somebody else. Like a note she's picked up from the table.

"Don't brake. You brake we'll go all over. Stay straight."

Ben glances at her. He nods, moves his foot away from the pedal.

In the center of the riverbed is a thin shoal of water. Cloudmirror. There's no avoiding it. She sees him aim for the shallowest part and ease the gas. They go ten miles an hour. Fifteen. She holds her breath, but the water folds away easy from the wheels. Ben keeps accelerating, and soon they rattle up and over the far bank. Maranda doesn't let go of the grab-handle, her knuckles still cracked and white.

BEN

He stops the car on the other side of the river and gets out. There's no sound but the wind. No birds, no cars, nothing. The Audi has mud halfway up its tires, dirtier than they've ever let it get, but other than that it seems okay.

Maranda's turned away from him, breathing heavily. He doesn't know what the hell's the matter with her now, but God it makes him anxious. He's anxious every second around her. She's made no attempt these last two days to hide how much she despises him.

If he's being honest, he'd wanted it to all be like the night she moved in with him, the first night, when they'd danced in the kitchen and everything was easy and right, when they knew exactly how to move. He'd left the light on over the sink and the room was small and close and the only music they needed was each other. When he stepped on her toes she laughed and pretended to fall, and of course he caught her.

"I'm high maintenance," she warned him, smirking.

He picked her back up and twirled her around. "I don't mind," he said. He could smell her hair, like laundry, like air and rain.

"I'm serious," she said. "Can you handle that? All of me?"

Why couldn't everything have stayed? She's nothing like that now, an entirely different woman. He hadn't expected *that* from marriage, surely.

He scratches his neck, thinking she probably feels the same about him. There were so many ways they'd kept themselves hidden. And no wonder. Getting close is handing over a dagger and turning your back.

Ben bites his lip, gets back in the car. Well, here they are. Maybe that's the price you pay.

Still, there was so much he should have noticed. Like the time she'd asked him to play something from his record collection.

"You pick," she'd said. "Something happy. I want to feel happy."

It had been a good day—they'd been out for dinner and he was starting to think he wanted to see her always. It was soon enough after they met that he was still quietly thrilled at the sight of her in his house.

He'd chuckled and handed her a drink, sipping from another as he walked his fingers across the sleeves. Most of his collection was from thrift shops but he'd bought a few new ones since vinyl went vogue again. He took one from a white sleeve and spun it around in his hand with a flourish and set it on the player.

She was already standing, eyes closed, moving her hips in anticipation of whatever music was coming, but as soon as it did, as soon as the first chords walked down the stairs, a frown crossed her face. She stopped dancing and opened her eyes, staring fixedly at a point across the room. Ben thought she was playing a game, but it kept going.

"Hey, Mar. Mar."

He shook her by the shoulder, but she wouldn't come out of it. He said her name again, this time a question.

They find their way back to Route 1.

They might be driving through the spirit-world. A hellscape. There's the smell of burn even with the air vents closed. Ben can feel the clamminess in his skin and hair. If they ever do emerge in Anchorage they'll do so with layers of soot caked on, plated and armored.

In places the asphalt has buckled up enormously. They have to use the shoulder to get by.

Honestly, he's hoping she'll give up and want to turn around soon. What are they doing out here anyway? It's almost a thousand miles from Juneau to Anchorage, all on Route 1, and they're making shit for time so far. He finds himself bitten by a profound torpor. You never make a dent in this kind of distance.

The forest to the east as far as they can see is flattened, blown down like it was little more than grass to be bent.

"What could have done this?" Maranda whispers.

He reaches for the radio without even thinking, then pauses. It feels like he's impeding on a stranger. Like she doesn't think he's worth the space he takes up. He's been trying to keep his movements small and innocuous, nothing that she might, even for a moment, be annoyed by. He's been folding his protein bar wrappers into neat squares and stuffing them into his pockets, even though hers are on the floor and down in the crevices of both doors.

He turns his head enough to make it known he's deferring to her.

"I don't care," she shrugs.

Incredibly, music strangles out. It's the first non-report they've gotten. The song's a few years old now, one that was starting to get big when they met. He's pretty sure it played on their first "date," actually.

He's not sure it should count as a date, given that they'd already fucked. The night they met they went back to his place, backed into a wall, pulling at each other's clothes.

"What's your name?" he'd asked, breathless. He was trying to get past her belt. But she hadn't answered. Just tongued her lip and smiled and inched back to let him.

It was a few nights later they went for a proper dinner. He can't remember the name of the place—why can't he remember the name? He feels a surge of guilt. He didn't take it seriously enough. He wasn't *there*. He was hardly ever, really, there.

All he does remember is the strangeness of having already done *that* and now trying to step into something tentative and liminal, like they were trying to legitimize it, but she didn't seem bothered at all. They'd talked about his work, her desire to head Outside soon. No talk of sex, no scurrilous banter, and so he figured that's how they were playing it. That this really was their first night. That what had already happened hadn't happened at all.

The engine starts making a kind of clattering rattle. The pedal goes half-responsive.

"Shit," Ben says, coming out of the memory. The car vibrates over the rumble-strips and crunches to a stop. He shuts it off and they sit there as the engine clicks and dings.

He sees her glance at him. She can pick up when he's overwhelmed or pissed off sometimes before he's even aware of it—like now. Then she clams up, which just pisses him off even more.

"All right," he mumbles, getting out.

Everything smells like campfire, close and dry. He lifts the hood, muttering to himself. He knows how to do a few things on a car but nowhere near enough. His father tinkered with engines, but he never trusted Ben to do anything more than hold the old part or retrieve a tool, so Ben picked up what he picked up, but how much was that?

Now, he looks at what's under the hood and it seems to him indecipherably smooth. Like it's all of one piece. There's little grime, less corrosion. He was hoping to see a loose cord, maybe, or a part he could thumb back in and that would do it.

Maranda gets out, turning in a slow circle.

Ben frowns. He can identify a few of the reservoirs, wiper fluid, engine coolant, brake fluid, but when he grabs a seemingly innocuous hose there's a sharp skin-hiss.

"Jesus Christ," he growls, shaking his hand.

He goes to punch the thing but stops. A hurricane rage closes around him, and he lets it blow a second—it feels good. Maranda's maybe forty feet away. Just standing there.

She's right in his line of sight, back to him, standing between two scrubbed-clean pines. She's frozen now, obviously scared by him.

Really? He can't even burn his goddamn hand?

She twists her neck out and takes a few steps, kind of splay-footed. He's almost certain she's somebody else already, probably the kid from the kitchen, Chipmunk.

She looks at one of the trees, then a different one. She turns around to face him and tilts her head way over.

"What happened to all the trees?" she asks.

He doesn't answer, going back to whatever's under the hood. She'll probably only be out for a minute anyway.

Everything is a uniform black. There's a reservoir of purple coolant. Probably the engine has flooded and it needs time, but he removes his button-down and uses it to dry a few of the cables, just in case. He wants to have done *something*. Then he stands there with his hands on his hips.

Chipmunk wanders further off, looking at the forest like it's a museum gallery.

"Hey!" Ben calls. "Where are you going?"

She screws up her face all the way up one side. "Dunno," she shrugs, and wanders further.

He grips the edge of the hood and squeezes for all he can. On top of everything else, it's too damn much. What exactly is his job here? To be not just the driver and mechanic and celibate husband but a babysitter too?

The hurricane's back upon him but he doesn't care. He disconnects the hood strut and slams it so hard it echoes.

Chipmunk immediately ducks, covering her ears.

"Come on," he barks. "We've got to keep going."

She trudges back to the car, her lower lip quivering. She climbs in with her shoulders curled forward, hands between her knees, and something falls in him. A tenderness.

He gentles the door shut, biting his lip. What the hell is he doing? What is he *supposed* to do with all this? He shakes his head, walking around to the car's other side. Maybe this was all doomed from the start.

MARANDA

All of a sudden she's out, in the car, and they're midway through a fight. She's got no idea what's been said, or where it's going. Just *boom*—and she's there. Good thing she's quick on her feet.

Whoever's been out, arguing, has Maranda half full of rage already. It's pulsing in her neck. Her mind feels electric, ready to strike.

"It was a mistake," Ben says. "It was an accident."

"An accident? It's not like you tripped. You had a *choice*, Ben."

A voice says: *Well* yeah *he had a choice. He knew what he was doing, you just aren't worth it.*

It's a wind strong enough to take dead leaves from a tree. It's the new voice, the one that leaves her cold. Whatever collected steam-rage has got her going collapses. Now all she wants to do is cry.

Guardian pushes the cold voice down and says: *Don't cry. You give that up and he'll only take more.*

"Why wasn't I worth it?" she says. "Why wasn't I worth it to you?"

"Look," he says, running a hand through his hair. "Look, I'm sorry. I don't know what else you want me to say."

Her whole life, *this* is the way things go: other people do whatever they want, and then she pays for it. They say they're sorry while she bleeds.

Sorry, Maranda. Sorry I wasted your life and, you know, married you while I was screwing other people. Sorry I never loved you because you weren't pretty enough.

Sorry I fucked you, kid.

She almost prefers people like her ex Luke, or Louise. There's no sorry there. They meant it, so they did it.

She's got backpacks of other people's sorries, while they walk around carrying nothing. Ben came clean, great. A weight got lifted off his shoulders and he's a new man and zip-a-dee-doo-da, but you know where that all went?

She rolls her eyes. "Yeah, well. Sorry doesn't really help me now."

"What would you like me to say, huh?" He smacks his thigh, and all the alarms go off. She can hear them yelling inside. Axel's voice comes through like a spear.

Fuck him. Fuck him. That's a goddamn pussy move.

She finds the rabbit in her jacket pocket and touches it until she regains some kind of calm, but Ben is still going.

"You weren't exactly the perfect little wifey, were you? *I* made all the money. *I* took care of everything around the house."

"I never worked?"

"Part-time. You didn't make enough to pay for anything." He tilts his head, indicating her watch.

"Oh nice. *Nice,* Ben." She fumbles it off and throws it at him. "Here. Here, have it. Maybe we can set up payment plans for the other shit, that way you aren't put out. Probably got lots of people to buy for anyway, huh?"

"You know what?" he says.

"What?"

"Maybe if you weren't so…"

"Yeah? Finish that."

But he doesn't say. Just pulls on his mouth and clenches.

She's a project to him. A crazy girl he can rescue. Bullshit. She didn't need rescuing then, and she still doesn't. She's not potential, and anyway maybe he ought to let her *agree* to his help. She's been on her own since before Ben was potty trained, practically.

She glares out the window. He's a jackass. There's so much surface he doesn't know, or even care to understand. So how could he handle the stuff she's hiding in her beehive of a mind?

The wind *cha-chunks* at the blanket over the windshield. The forest is a gray spectrograph beyond the glass. It makes her remember, just for a second, that one restaurant where the walls had been painted like a forest. Now, there's probably less green in a hundred miles than there was on that wall.

Up until that date, it felt like her whole life had been smoke. Her brain a cloud that would blow away any minute. But when Ben looked up from his plate she felt like part of his hunger, and that meant she was solid and substantial and real. But now even her few good memories have turned to bad ones. No matter how far they drive, she'll never be able to outrun that simple fact.

She thought he had seen her, really seen her. Loved her, even. Like the night he'd danced her around the kitchen, into the small hours of the night. He spun her around and he smelled like the earth. She was safe. When she asked if he could handle all of her, hadn't he said yes?

When they pass a lone tree still standing alongside the road, she has no trouble imagining the yank of a good noose around her neck. There are so many ways you could die. With your underwear hot and blood-soaked. A car going slow-motion over your skull.

Maybe she'll deflate. Maybe she'll shatter into a million knives of glass.

As night starts falling, Ben pulls the Audi off the road, way back in the dead growth. The headlights slant into the trees. Then everything's dark but the sky, a sludge-paste of red and purple.

He inches the front seat forward and offers her the back with a nod. Won't talk. Whatever. She unfurls a few blankets and tries to settle in.

"Enough room?" he says.

"I'm fine."

There's a moment of quiet in her mind. No past peeking through. She could be thankful, but she knows better. Quiet is just the yellow before a storm.

BEN

The dark is closer than vision. Ben wakes to the sound of a grunt-moan from the backseat but can't tell if he dreamed it. There's a breath of silence, then the noises start again.

"No…*nha*…No!"

He clicks on the dome light to find Maranda writhing under her blankets. One foot kicks half-heartedly at the door. Her arms are over her head, hands clenching and unclenching.

"Please," she's saying. "*Unnh.*"

He reaches back for her, sees her belly rhythmically distending. She starts crying now, too.

"Mar." He climbs over the center console. "Mar, wake up. Mar."

He starts shaking her, but she doesn't stop. Her hands are still above her head. Her stomach lurches and moves.

"Mar! Hey!"

He has the insane thought that forcing her arms back to their regular position will restore her to normal, but when he tries she raises them back up with a strength he knows for a fact she doesn't have, and the sleeves slide away from her hands.

"What the hell?" he whispers.

The skin on both wrists is bright and raw. Like a scald. Suddenly she sits upright, gasping. He half expects her to vomit. Her eyes are bolted, clear as anything in the dark.

"Mar?"

She kicks the blankets from her lap, casting about. She keeps pulling at her wrists, like she's ripping snakes from them, first one and then the other, grabbing and throwing.

Ben's so freaked out it sounds like anger. "Mar! Hey, Mar! Mar!"

She scrambles against the door, pure terror. No idea Ben was even there before he spoke. He has the sense she's only seeing him through a tunnel, at some insane remove from reality.

"It's me." He does his best to sound reassuring, even though he's all but fully panicked now. "You're okay. It's me."

She leans down and groans, holding her stomach. She stays like that, completely still. It seems for a moment—he actually thinks this—that she has leaked all the way to death, that this noise was her spirit evacuating, but then he sees her chest lift, thank God. He's about to pull a blanket over her, but as soon as he touches her knee she startles awake again and her arm slaps out and gropes for the handle.

She half-stumbles into the night, taking off into the woods. Ben follows.

It's vacuum-silent out here, outer-fucking-space. No insects or life-noise at all. Even the sound of their footfalls is curiously deadened. The forest is a graveyard of trunks, some of them cracked halfway up, leaning like broken fingers.

"Mar. Maranda!"

It's not until he can see the paleness of her arms that he realizes how damn cold it is. A chill that slices under the skin. She's holding her elbows and turning like a lost child. Then she stops, wavering on her feet. He catches her by the shoulders, but she gasps and tries to pull herself away.

For the first time he's genuinely, truly, afraid. Not of her or the guys who shot at them, or of Axel or the scorch, but of where she's been. Of the freight train that's barreling toward them out of the past. It's too much. It's going to run them down.

He holds her face, but she's looking everywhere else, like the air is flaming with a fire only she can see. "Mar. Mar, it's me. It's me!"

Suddenly, her mouth tightens. Her eyes narrow to slits, looking over his shoulder at nothing. Then her eyes roll back and she's herself again.

"What the hell is going on?" he whispers.

Finally, she sees him. It's like a plug gets pulled and whatever she's been seeing circles the drain. He expects her to collapse into him, he's almost craving that, but instead she squirms away and heads for the car.

A maw opens up in his belly, a wallowing hopelessness. He's a fool, a fucking idiot. What's he supposed to do with all this? How's he supposed to help when she's more afraid of him than of *it*?

He watches in the direction she's gone, but it's all black. She slams the door so hard he flinches.

The man in the blue blazer stands over the black waters of the Gastineau as the ferry ghosts across. No other vessels to be seen. To the east, the mountains look like the back of a sleeping dragon. You can all but see the heartbeat, like it might lumber awake at any moment and shake rocky accumulate from its bones.

He's picking at something in his hand, dropping pieces to the deck as Juneau falls away behind them. It's mostly lightless, buildings only hints of shadow against a deeper black. Here and there is a wash of red and blue emergency lights, but soon even this disappears, and the city fades to nothingness.

"Hey! Hey!"

Behind him, his unshaven partner is up on the bridge with a young captain, who's doubled over and bleeding from his nose. His partner laughs, punches the captain again, and waves.

The blazered man drops what's in his hand but doesn't wave back. He brushes his palm against his jeans. Moving spasmodically on the deck is a now-legless, wingless, and antenna-less grasshopper.

MARANDA

They drive the morning through, accompanied by quiet so thick you could cut slices off for a sandwich.

After last night, little snippets of the past keep bleeding through. She's trying not to think about them, but it's not working.

The image of her father's house so small behind her. $13.25 in her pocket, no change of clothes, figuring maybe four hours before he'd be sober enough to notice or give coherent chase. Beating her fists into her thighs to stay warm, flinching every time a car shushed by, thinking even weeks later it was going to be him, his fingers pinching her bicep to the bone.

Her memory's broken slivers. Each one tiny. Each one knife-sharp.

A man with shopping bags on his feet, taking her by the wrist. Nights in the park, people on benches flashing lighters in their palms. Like a rock concert, like Christmas Eve. Later, on a bus, she rides and rides. An open spot in the floor where the road showed through, and all she could think about is how fast it would sand her down. If she put her face to it, how quickly you'd see bone.

A man she swears she's never seen on top of her. The faces he's making. She wants to turn away, but the cold voice tells her to stop pretending to be something she's not.

Shut up, she thinks.

They stop within view of the border crossing at Pleasant Camp, back far enough to watch and wait. It's a brown building with an awning over two lanes. A white pickup parked in the back. There aren't any lights on but there don't seem to be lights anywhere now, so you can't tell.

Ben watches through the binoculars. Maranda shuffles their papers in her lap. She goes back and forth between watching the building and watching Ben.

She's not afraid of what's outside. Not that she's brave, there's just nothing she's not expecting. Death can get you in so many ways. Your body slo-mo through a windshield. Glass finger-peeling you through. She imagines herself hitting the pavement and skidding with a force that pulls muscle from bone. She's not afraid of any of it.

For five years she watched for her father on the street. Waited for it to be him on the phone. Hell, for him to walk in, lay down the money, and start doing it all over again. Then one day she opened up the Daily and there he was, dead. She'd expected relief but nothing changed. That's when she realized that he could, and did, still walk into her mind and do it anytime.

That's what she's really afraid of: her own mind turning against her. Which it does all the fucking time.

She tries to think about Gracie. Gracie's the only good thing she's got in her head. Sometimes, she'd come back for the day and could tell Gracie was nearby. There'd be brightness in the air, a clarity. And sure enough, there'd she'd be, either coloring on Maranda's bed or already sleeping under the covers. Once she drew hearts with a red-ballpoint and left them everywhere, all over the floor.

Eventually Ben puts the binoculars down and shrugs, starting the car.

There's only one guy manning the border. He gives their papers a once over and waves them into the Yukon, shaking his head.

"Good luck," he half-laughs.

They've finished off the second of their three red cans of fuel when they see a place past Haines Junction that still has its lights on. A two-pump station with an Airstream trailer in the back. The only other one they've seen was a day ago, and that was shut down and padlocked.

Ben gets out of the car, twisting out his back. "You see that?" he says.

She feels fuzzy but has no idea why. She can't hear right. Like water's surrounding her brain, echoing and slubbing in her ears. The voices are louder, too.

Ben is looking at her, waiting.

"What?" she blinks. "Sorry."

He fumbles in his back pocket for the credit card, jerks his chin up at the pasted-on sign. "I said, you believe that?"

The price is nearly tripled from what it was a few days ago, but she can't find it in herself to care. She's too busy with her own head. Right now the voices are talking mainly to each other. It's like being drunk at a dinner, catching only snippets of conversation.

Axel says: *You say that again…oh, you have no idea. None.*

Someone wants cigarettes. *Would kill for them.* That one's Klara, she's pretty sure, every word is curled and accented. She's known about Klara for a while.

Somebody else is crying. Just crying.

Ben smacks the machine.

"Come on," he whines at it. "Son of a bitch."

There's a couple seconds missing. Couldn't have been more. His card won't read, and she's standing exactly where she was before.

Suddenly though, she feels more assured, more at home in her body. She stands up straighter, has the distinct feeling that soon she'll sprout wings.

Ben's puts his card back in his wallet. He starts for the door, but she holds a hand up to stop him.

"Cool down," she says. "I got it." There's something extra, a weighty spring in her voice. Somebody else—Klara, probably—is just under the surface. She doesn't even bother to wait to see if he'll listen to her. She checks her eyes in her phone's reflection and pulls the zipper down from her throat.

Slowly, everything moves further and further away.

She can feel herself walking different. Strutting her ass. The bell chimes as she enters the store, high, small, silver. Bells are always chiming if you listen.

Maranda's only able to watch as the man behind the counter looks up. She tries to move, tries to say something, but Klara's out now and she can't.

The man eyes her up and down, and you can tell he hears the bells too. Klara applies lipstick, and the guy watches that too. First one side, then the other. It feels very good, very right. Like he's a charmed snake, and she's moving him this way and that. You have to make a snake forget what it is, that's the way to keep it from putting its venom in you.

She checks her lipstick in the reflection on her phone, and there's an unlit Marlboro between her middle and index fingers. She finds herself with an incredible craving for menthols.

"It seems the pump will not work," her mouth—*Klara's* mouth—says. "Our card."

The man nods. "Afraid we're cash only for the foreseeable future."

"But I have no cash," Klara says. A pause. "There must be *something* we can do."

Maranda's uncomfortable. But at the same time, when she looks at him, a little thrill-bubble pops behind her navel. She can see hunger swim his body like a whale through sea. It moves from his eyes and under his mouth and down, past his chest and his belly and into the deep waters. He glances at her breasts. She feels suddenly dumb for ever having sex with Ben without getting anything back. Just giving it away.

The words come out of her mouth low and close, Klara's voice, no volition on Maranda's part. "I'll show them to you. This is fair?"

As the guy clears his throat and sniffs, Maranda starts clamoring, trying to get back in control, but it doesn't happen. She watches the guy shrug and indicate the magazines. "I can see titties anytime I want."

Okay, Maranda thinks. *Okay, enough now.*

Klara's voice: *Sorry dear. Everyone else has their turn. This is mine. Plus, you need gas, and the world is not a charity.*

"You cannot touch the ones in magazines, can you?"

The man's eyebrows lift. "No."

Maranda tries to force words out of her own mouth, but nothing comes.

Seriously Klara, enough.

No, Klara says. *There is blood in the water.*

Klara sets the phone down on the counter. She leans close, squeezing her elbows a little.

Maranda's getting pushed out of the way, she can tell. She can only half-hear things. It feels like she's falling asleep.

"Twenty seconds," she hears Klara say. "And Menthols."

The man swallows. Things are getting darker. The last she knows Klara's hand is undoing the top button of Maranda's shirt, and the man's tongue is moving like a little bird over his teeth.

BEN

When Maranda finally returns, they're able to get enough to fill the tank and one of the red containers. She's got a smirk on her face but won't say anything about it. They drive the rest of the afternoon in silence.

Later, she sniffs and looks around, like she's forgotten where she is. She pats at her pockets and leans down, reaching into the cracks around the seat.

"What?" he asks.

"Where's my phone?"

"Your phone?"

"Yeah."

"Shit, Maranda. We need that."

She stares at him, open-mouthed, like *you think?* "I had it this morning."

"Well—where is it now?"

"Ben, if I knew I wouldn't be, you know, fucking looking for it."

How is this on him? How is this something else he also has to solve? "Should we go back?"

"I don't..." But then she shakes her head, suddenly decisive. "No. No, it's—too far. It might not even be there anyway."

"That's great. That's great, Mar. Now we have zero phones. Thank you. That's very helpful."

"What are you talking about, zero phones? You've got yours."

"I…" He'd forgotten he hadn't told her. "I left my charger at the house."

He can feel her glaring. He's expecting her to lay into him, but she doesn't say anything. It goes on so long he glances over, hoping she's zoned out or whatever.

"You're a dick," she announces.

He sighs, goes back to watching the road. She's probably right. He doesn't respond and, eventually, she falls asleep.

That's what she does: when things get to be too much she either flies into a rage or falls asleep. Once, he got home and found her lying in the shower, the water gone cold. She looked dead, but when he turned the water off and touched her shoulder her hands shot out, sharp and sudden. It took her a few seconds to even realize she was cold and let herself be toweled off.

There had been other signs, things he maybe could have, or *should have,* seen, but when he'd asked her, later, about the shower, she'd shrugged and mumbled something noncommittal. Eventually he just let it go.

He hasn't been able to stop thinking about the marks on her wrists, though. What's he supposed to *do* against something like that?

They're driving on Mars. It's hard to imagine that things will ever grow back right again. Already, the memory of anything not dry and sepia-scorched is fading. The way things were—

what, two, three days ago?—feels less than real, and he's getting the feeling they won't be back to their house anytime soon. If ever.

Strange, how quickly you accept despair. How quickly anything else becomes just wishful thinking.

When they stop to eat, he finds a single strip of untouched grass a few yards back from the road. It's small, maybe twice as long as the car, and surrounded on all sides by dirt and brittle-burn. He wants to remove his boots and run his toes through the grass, to remember how it feels, but he can't quite bring himself to. Like this smallest blessing is too frangible to do anything but fear.

At any moment, the sky might scroll away. At any moment you might look up and see the raw mouth of God.

It makes Ben think about his father, even though he's been dead for years. The man talked all the goddamn time about the Rapture, about the faithful being spirited away, leaving behind their clothes, watches, fillings—that and the wicked, of course. It would happen instantaneously, he insisted, without fanfare. As a boy, Ben would lie awake at night and if he could not hear his father moving, breathing, snoring, he would eventually creep from his bed to make sure he was still there.

Once, he came home and his dad, gone for a meeting, had laid out unfolded clothes for the next day. It looked like he'd been zapped right out of them. The terror of that still occasionally resurrects, even though Ben doesn't believe a word of it anymore. He can't help it. From time to time, he still finds himself watching the clouds.

There's maybe an hour left of daylight. A hell haze to the north. Ben has his door open, his father's New Testament in his lap. His eyes continue scraping the same line word by word. The radio is on, crackling.

"*...blast radius did not reach Anchorage...relief efforts...flights and ships are grounded indefinitely...cause of the Yukon disaster still unknown.*"

He sighs. The verses are all things he's read and heard a hundred times before. It goes over him like clouds. He tries another page near the back.

"*...FEMA has established Anchorage as a safe zone...*"

Maranda comes out of the woods, zipping her fly. She takes a bottle of water from the roof and splashes some on her hands, flicking her fingers.

Ben's doesn't want it to seem like he's hiding anything, so he waits until she drops herself roughly into the passenger seat before he closes and deposits the book in the back.

"Why...*why?*" she asks, motioning.

He starts the car and the engine ropes over. "I really don't know."

He can feel her staring. He studies dust on the dash, but the discomfort of being watched elongates, until finally she shrugs, settles back, and he pulls them onto the road.

It's so damn awkward. How did everything get so awkward?

The road is completely empty. Split through in places. There are lava-cracks a foot wide.

The radio's gone mostly to static, so he shuts it off. "Sounds like Anchorage may be a little crowded," he says.

She leans her head against the window, looking at the sky. "It's bad out there."

"Yeah."

She turns to him, frowns. "What?"

Ben shrugs, but his wife's a bloodhound. He knows she'll drill to bone.

"What are you thinking?" she asks.

He wipes his mouth. He feels like an actor in his own life—conscious of everything he does and how it appears to her. "Just…Dad was big on the judgment of God business. Rapture stuff. You know, the Big Sheriff wiping out, like, all evil with his right hand."

"Sounds charming."

"Yeah."

"When did he…?"

"I was in grad school. Heart attack."

She nods. "I knew about your mom, but I don't think I knew that."

Ben sighs. "Dad wasn't a fun man. And all that…it leaves a mark."

She raises her eyebrows. "Tell me about it." She looks at him with something like pity, maybe, then motions out the window at the parade of 60 mile-an-hour destruction. "What would he say about all this?"

"Something like, who cares? He was on the first flight out."

It's fast becoming dark. There's fire light above the trees. Up ahead, a pine has broken off halfway up its trunk and fallen across the road, catching in the branches across the way. There's room for them to drive right underneath.

"So, what?" Maranda says. "Now you think fire's gonna rain down from the sky?"

"I mean, it already did."

She laughs. "Touché."

He's nearly grounded by the certainty that if he says more, if he gives her anything of himself, she'll despise it, but he wants to be honest. There's more he wants to say. He takes a breath, gathering. "I mean, maybe there's something to it. Not the end, I don't know. Just, I want to get myself…" He glances at her. She's looking back, attentive, and for the briefest moment it feels like there's nothing standing between them. "…turned around, before it's any later."

Slowly, Maranda nods. "I don't really know what to do with that," she says.

"Mar, listen, I…"

The car jolts. Containers in the back thump up and back down. They fishtail, just for a second, until Ben mad-grips the wheel straight.

Maranda loses focus, cracks her neck, but shakes it off. She's got one hand on the dash. "What the hell was that?" she says.

"I don't know," he says. "We hit something."

"You don't know, or we hit something?"

"I don't know."

"Aren't you going to turn around?"

"It's driving fine," he shrugs. "It could've been anything. Could've been a…a stick or something."

She blinks at him, then crosses her arms. It's a ridiculously adolescent gesture. "A stick?"

"What?" Ben clips.

She doesn't answer. This is going to turn into some big deal, he can already tell. He feels momentarily beset by whoever or whatever is in control of his sad little life.

"*What?*"

"Whatever you want to do, right? Whatever *Ben* wants to do."

"Oh Jesus."

He hits the brakes too hard. The tires squeal. He sees her scare, and he's sickly pleased about it. He U-turns as violently as he possibly can.

"Yeah, exactly. Driving to Anchorage in the middle of a natural disaster is exactly the way I want to spend my Saturday, thank you. And, you know, with no idea why."

"You didn't have to come."

He bites the inside of his cheeks. He's losing his mind. Trying to have any kind of reasonable conversation with her is going to turn him into a crippled, slobbering idiot.

The road materializes out of the headlights. It's almost fully dark now. Splayed firelight crowns the windshield. Maranda leans up, both palms on the dash.

"Here," she whispers.

Sure enough, there's a shape in the road. No bigger than a purse. She unclips her seatbelt.

"No, *please*," Ben says. "Please, allow me."

He's half hoping for a fight here, for a chance to be angry, but she just shrugs and settles back in. He exits the car in a huff.

Outside, at the edge of the headlights, he pauses. You can feel sheer enormity surrounding them, a howling void. Everything is ancient again, frayed at the edges.

This is only the beginning, he thinks. They have no idea. Not yet.

Ben shakes his head, returns to his own self. He crouches, forearms on his knees, to see what he's killed.

The dome light clicks on as he re-enters the car.

"What was it?" Maranda asks.

"Just a rabbit."

He sits and closes the door behind him. Goes to start the car.

"What?"

"It was just a rabbit."

"You hit a bunny?"

"Yeah, it was a rabbit."

"Why the hell did you hit a bunny?"

"It…" Goddamnit. He's going to lose his mind. "It ran in front of me. I didn't run the thing down for Christ's sake."

"You hit a bunny! If you weren't driving like…"

"Listen, the dumb thing ran out. It made a beeline for my tire and put its, like, stupid head under it."

She covers her mouth. Something in her face breaks and falls.

"Okay, I shouldn't have—"

She opens the door.

"What are you doing? Jesus, Mar, it's just a—"

But it slams before he can finish. The light blinks out. He grabs two handfuls of his own hair and bites back a yell. Maranda marches away from the car, wiping her eyes with the heel of her hand as she kicks through the chaparral, eventually coming up with a branch. Then she kneels down in the road and just looks at the thing. Like it's going to hop up if she empathizes with it enough.

Is she *talking* to it?

He'd assumed she was going to sort of spatula the thing out of the road, but no, of course not. Instead she tucks the stick under her arm and grabs the thing by two forelegs and awkwardly cradles it away from the road, where she starts scratching in the dirt. After a minute she stops to wipe her mouth on her wrist. Then keeps at it.

Jesus. Just…Jesus.

He's got no idea what he's supposed to do. He can't for a second understand how her mind works or figure out what the hell she wants. But then again maybe she's right—maybe he's just a dick.

He gets out of the car and eases the door shut behind him. The air is so close it gets into your clothes. Fire-wind. The day's heat ebbs back from the roof of the car. He shuffles around with his boots until he finds a flat rock and kicks at it until he gets a corner and can wedge it up. It's big enough. Wieldable.

When he walks up behind her, he doesn't say anything and neither does she. He bends beside the two-inch trench she's begun and starts stone-shoveling. Dirt gets in his socks. He keeps his head down, but he can feel her watching him. Then, slowly, she starts digging again too.

Outside Haines Junction, there's a single tree fallen adjacent to the filling station, and a giant shelf of uprooted earth. An Airstream trailer's still out back.

At the pump, the blue-blazered guy walks back and forth in front of the Pilot, squinting at his phone, holding it up and taking a few steps and then holding it out further. His jacket is impossibly clean. The younger guy peels back his lower lip and thumbs in a plug of snuff as he walks toward the store.

"It's me," the blazered guy finally says, glancing up as the door-chime sounds. "It's hell out here. We're driving through hell."

"Okay," she says.

"I want more. Normal price was for normal circumstances. These are not."

"You already agreed."

"Yeah, well," he rotates a shoulder. "Maybe we're changing our minds."

Through the phone, he can hear her breathing through her nose. He leans against the hood of the car and declines to initiate whatever comes next. He checks the underside of one boot, then the other. Through the store window he can see his partner approaching the counter, where the fat proprietor has his feet up and a smut rag folded back, tilting his head, adjusting his glasses.

"Okay, how about this," she says. "How about this. That thing you want to try on one of our girls. I keep saying no."

He puts the foot down. He stands up straighter. In the store, his unwashed partner is waving his arms. The proprietor does the same. Their voices are muffled.

"I'm listening," he says.

"That. You bring her in. I'll let you try it."

"On her."

The sound of his boss laughing is somehow wet and dry at once. Nicotined. "You sick fuck," she says. "Fine. On her."

"Deal."

He hangs up. He walks around the vehicle, kicking at the tires. Then he leans against the hood and waits.

The trees are covered in ash and leaning crazily across what now seems to be a wintered forest. A good quarter of them have fallen already. The whole world has bent to the point of breaking.

Suddenly, there's a cymbal crash. He has time to see the proprietor in mid-air, his arms and legs akimbo and shards of glass suspended all around him. The guy hits the ground and half-somersaults back over his head, then flops the rest of the way. There's blood in his eyes, and as he crab-walks away from the store a hand shoots from under him and you can hear the *sing* of glass on asphalt as it happens. He raises a sliced palm, blood runneling down to the elbow. He tries to get his legs beneath him but can't.

His partner kicks the door open, and the frame bell dings. "Now?" he yells. "Got a clearer picture now, shitwipe?"

The man scrambles to his feet, slides once, and takes off down the road.

The younger man whoops. "Right behind ya right behind ya right behind ya!" He holds his knees and cackles until the blue-blazered guy punches him in the shoulder.

"What?" He starts laughing again. "Shit, man." He waggles a cell phone with a night-blue cover. "Lookee what I found."

MARANDA

She's in and out more. Fuzzy. She can't stop thinking about whatever happened at the filling station. That guy with the tongue. God, she feels the kind of befouled you can't wash off.

That wasn't her, though. It's different what Ben did. She didn't want it, doesn't even know what the hell happened.

Still though, she can't get his face out of her head.

There's something else too. A memory trying to pry its way in. It feels like—if it ever does—that her brain will explode into confetti, into streamers of blood.

Two or three times this morning she's found herself asking Ben to repeat himself, going, "*What?*" until by now he's just stopped talking. Whatever. He's a goddamn boy. Needs everybody to like him, laugh at every joke, come twice a night during sex. All the time, she catches him watching her out the corner of his eye to see how she's reacting. Well, if he wants to pout, he can. Distance feels like the best option anyway.

They stop mid-morning to eat. Only the basics. Swigs of warm water. One protein bar a piece. The cans they save for the evening, spooning right out of the tin.

Ben tops off the tank from one of the newly filled canisters. She walks around a bit, stretching her legs. There's a silence over everything. The air charged with potential.

The sun is starting to try in the east, mostly hidden behind smoke, but you can maybe smell living things in the air again. She's turned, about to say this out loud, when everything shakes.

She assumes it's in her head, but then she notices the gas nozzle bumping side to side off the collar, and at the same time Ben repeating the word "shit" to himself. He puts a hand on the window for balance. The whole car jostles.

Suddenly she's on the ground. Kneeling. Both hands pressed to the Earth like some kind of healer. She can hear, not far off, the snap of branches and the long groan of a toppling tree.

For a single second, she forgets to hold the past at bay, and when she blinks she sees a darkened TV in a hotel room. She's facing the blank screen, and she's so *there* she can smell lemon disinfectant. Fabric scrunching under her hands and knees. Someone is behind her and god it hurts, the pain is chasing her into the screen where she's reflected, her face zooming in and out. It's the black of space—the pain trying to push her in to where she'll fall forever.

When she opens her eyes, everything is still again. Her heart is a bird. Ben's watching her, eyebrows knit.

"Alright," he whispers. "You're alright."

He keeps saying it and saying it, as if that will make it true.

They drive through miles of burn. The road is lined with fallen trees, bald of green, and every so often one still afire trailing sparks into the air. She has no memory of even getting back into the car. Was someone else here, or did Ben have to lift her zombie-like into her seat? She wants to ask, but she also doesn't want to know.

"Look," Ben says after a while. "Look, I'm…I'm sorry. For what I said last night, about the rabbit. How I acted. For…just for everything."

She shifts uncomfortably.

Ben indicates with a nod the ruined world outside. "This is all…Well, I'm realizing things. About myself. I swung a long way from, like, Dad, all the God stuff. And, I don't know, not that I'm *for* it now, but…" He takes a breath. "I'm just saying I'd like to try to do things right."

Tension's coming off him in waves. When he looks at her she can tell he wants her to say something, to let him off the hook, but she wants to see where he'll go.

"It's just, what I was doing. Cheating on you. I thought nothing was, like, inherently bad. And I can see that's shit now. And it was, I don't know, I don't know another word, it was pathetic. Absolutely pathetic. And paying for it was…"

She has time to see his breath catch as he realizes his mistake.

He paid for it.

He won't look at her. He's looking straight ahead, but his eyes are going back and forth on the road.

He said he paid for it.

He paid for it.

Flashes of the past claw at the holes in her skull. Faces stripped of their names. A centipede burrowing her brain, each segment another john. Now, Ben.

She can't. Not now, after everything. She tries to hide from it, but sheaves of the earth begin falling away from her feet.

She hears *WHAT?* come out of her mouth, her voice suddenly with all the edge and bite of broken glass.

It's like she watches the rest through a curtain of storm. Everything's thrashing, windblown and rage-wild. She feels Axel's mind trying to break out of its cage.

Just when you think you've reached the end of Ben's shit.

The car's stopped, and they're both outside. She watches herself march him into the woods while he does all kinds of backpedaling, going, "No no no no no."

Lightning's branching her veins. It feels good. Feels real good. In her ribcage, every breath is an octopus. Alive. Tentacling down her arms, legs. Pure electric. Could power a whole town.

Not again, she hears. *Not. Again.*

A hurricane of knives, that's what Axel is. She's not positive, but she's pretty sure she just took a swing at Ben.

Her chest crackles. Swear to god you can smell ozone.

Now Ben's running, and he makes it about five steps before he slips in the leaves and she's on him—Axel's on him—lifting by the back of his shirt, shoving him. Throwing. He goes face-first into the ground, like he's sliding into second.

She's got lightning in her hands. Could piss a hole in steel.

Ben looks at her, awed, waiting for whatever hell's coming down.

"You need to decide if you're on Maranda's side or not," Axel growls. "And you need to decide *yesterday*."

The octopus crackles. Everything outside is blurry and humming.

Clicking on the dome light, he lights a menthol and rubs his cheeks, slaps himself. He has his jacket folded in his lap, the unstained Oxford unbuttoned enough to see tattoos on his collarbone.

The younger guy glances over, goes back to driving. There's no music, no radio, nobody speaks. On the dash is a copy of *The Ghoul Keepers.*

He retrieves a manila envelope from the glove compartment. Undoes the clasp and pulls out an old shot of Maranda flirt-pouting. She's recognizable, but only if you look hard. She's heavily made up, her hair blonde and past her shoulders, curled just the right way.

As he drives, the younger guy's also scrolling through the blue phone. It only took him an hour to unlock it. The blazered guy watches him, then takes the cigarette out. He opens his mouth wide, trying to pop his jaw.

BEN

Driving, Ben glances furtively at his wife, who has her forehead against the window.

She'd switched back standing above him, a few hours ago now, but ever since they got back in the car, he hasn't been able to keep still.

He'd thought Axel was going to kill him. Honestly, he'd thought that was it.

His arms are shaky and loose. He keeps fiddling with his jeans, the buttons on the dash. There's an anxiety star spreading out through the middle of his chest. But he didn't run, did he? No, he didn't beg. He'd looked death square in the face, which just happened to be the face of his wife.

He keeps glancing over. He wants to be ready, but has no idea what to even be ready for.

It's not a new feeling. She's always been all over the place. At times engaged, clingy. She once showed up at midnight in sweats and a winter jacket saying she couldn't sleep. Nothing funny, not a booty call or anything, but could she sleep on his couch? But then other times, like when she got pissed, she'd just disappear. Once she didn't return any of his calls for *three days*; he wasn't even sure if they were still together or not. When she finally called it was casual, just to say hey, did he want to get together later? Like nothing at all was wrong.

Now, she's not saying anything, and he sure as hell isn't talking. Not long after they got in the car, her anger—or was it Axel's anger?—got replaced by a torpor that's now brought her to the brink of non-responsiveness.

Still though, how's he supposed to feel about the fact that his wife—or someone in his wife—would threaten him like that? *He's* insane. He's the crazy one.

Sighing, he takes out his phone. It's blinking at 5% and there's a weak signal now, but who's he going to call anyway?

The roads seem to be getting worse. They pass an unidentifiable concrete mass—maybe a utilities bunker—but it's mostly gone. The exposed rebars are all swept in one direction, like hair blown underwater. He's hoping they're near the worst of it, that it'll recede as they approach Anchorage. But he can't offer anything logical. For all he knows it'll only get worse.

Enormous fires growl on the mountains. He clicks the wipers and they scoop ash into a little runnel on the side, a skinny pile that bit by bit blows away.

The road unspools into fog. The highway is fenced in with netting. As they pass Maranda watches it and says nothing, asks nothing, which Ben appreciates since he has no idea either.

The sudden ringing of his phone about stops his heart. The noise is obscene in the quiet.

"Jesus," he says, fumbling it out.

Maranda frowns. "Who is it?"

He glances, then makes eye contact with her. "Says it's you."

"Don't answer it," she says hurriedly, but he already has.

"Hello?"

On the other end, there's only static, then breathing. The rhythmic throb of tires. Ben can maybe hear something moving in the background.

"Hello? Hello? Who is—"

The other person gives a short exhalation, like they're amused, then the call beeps twice and dies. There's a dead battery center-screen.

"Who was that?" Maranda asks. Her voice is shaky, a whisper. He can feel her watching him, waiting for him to answer, but he doesn't. He's not sure why, but he can hardly breathe. Can hardly even think.

They round a bend, but the road ahead is entirely engulfed in flame. It looks like the literal gates of hell. They can feel heat even a quarter mile away.

The sky is an improbable color and the flames are whipping into the air like tentacles, like some kraken set to the ground and tortured. Ben glances, but Maranda's watching completely without affect.

"I saw a back road," he says, compelled to whisper. It feels like he could accidentally summon the fire's attention. "I don't know, maybe ten miles back."

"Okay."

They head back the way they came. Through the rear windshield, patched with flannel and duct tape, is a warbling orange glow.

Sure enough, there's an old pass through the mountains. Here too, smoke is over everything, a visible wave encroaching through the trees. The road cuts deep into a cliff. Maranda cranes her neck to look out the window, where the rock disappears above them like a waterfall of gray. Maybe somewhere up there a fire. Maybe somewhere the sun.

He watches her reflection in the window and tries to collect something worth saying, but whatever he comes up with evaporates into inadequacy as soon as he imagines the way she'd respond. She has a tenacious bullshit meter—she can see through even the most mundane, innocuous gesture to the undergirding core of selfishness, and goddamnit if she isn't usually right. He used to love that, back before it got turned on him.

When Ben finally does speak, he tries to turn the conversation back to Axel.

"I thought he was going to…I thought Axel was going to do it. He said I had to decide if I was on your side or not. And I had to decide right then. You don't remember."

It's not a question, he just wants to see if she'll admit it.

For a second, it crosses his mind that she could be faking all this—the people, the voices, the personality changes—but then he remembers, *really* remembers, the way Axel, an inch shorter and forty pounds lighter than Ben, had overpowered him in a second. The doubt passes as quickly as it came, and guilt and six other demons move in to take its place. They sit in his chest and arms, like he's filled with bathwater that won't drain.

You can't see the mountain at all, but you can feel its presence. Ben flicks the high beams on and whiteness immediately smothers the windshield. He switches them back off and glances at his wife.

"What?" he asks.

She gathers herself. Like she's been off somewhere else. "Are you?"

"Am I what?"

"Nevermind."

This is why—*this* is why he never gets close. All she does is jab. Before, he'd stayed in relationships as long as the girl seemed content at arm's length, and from the beginning, he could tell Maranda was mostly looking for shelter. It should've been easy. Plus, he'd get to be the good guy, white horse and all that. What happened out of town was his own business—it allowed him to have his head on straight when they were together. She was better off because of it, and what she didn't know didn't exist.

Now though, there's no such thing as distance, is there? Only near-constant anxiety.

He maneuvers the steering wheel with his index and middle fingers. He's trying to unscrew a water bottle when he notices two smears of white in the rearview mirror.

"Shit." He grabs the mirror and swivels it. Sure enough, only a hundred yards away, maybe less, are headlights. Small and indistinct in the smoke, but definitely there.

"What is it?"

"Shit," he repeats. There's nowhere to turn off. No other roads. And no chance of outrunning anybody here. He slows down and pulls onto the shoulder, reaching back and fumbling for the backpack. He keeps thinking about the call—the bemused chuckle—coming from Maranda's phone.

"What is it?" she says again. Her voice is sharp until she notices the gun.

"Someone's behind us," Ben says.

He has his hand on the door. Maranda's eyes close and her head tracks right to left, but he doesn't wait to see if someone else switches in.

Outside, the air is unseasonably warm. It folds around his shape, like a curtain he parts with his body. He stands behind the open door like he imagines he's supposed to, like he's seen in movies. If someone shoots through the window the bullet's going to enter his gut or his dick but he doesn't know how else to stand. He's trying not to think about the way he froze in Juneau.

It's probably nothing. Most certainly probably nothing. But the phone call—who *was* that? Truthfully, there's nothing to stop a person if they decide they want your food or your money. To tie you up and rape your wife in front of you.

The haze is so thick that he can't see the car, but he can hear the brakes squeal. Smoke drifts in slow currents over the headlights.

God his heart is going. He glances into the Audi— Maranda is squatting on the floor with her fingertips on the passenger seat. It looks like it's one of the alters now,

Guardian maybe, flexed and watching Ben like he's the starter pistol.

He takes one hand from the gun and wipes it on his jeans. Invisibly, a door opens and shuts. The air moves through trees. There's the staticky sound of distant fire.

Ben's voice is tight. "Hello?" He tries to sound more at ease, more confident, than he actually is.

All that comes back is a cough, warm and productive.

"You following us?" Ben calls.

The engine lopes, belt squeaking. "Look," the voice says. "Look, I ain't aiming to hurt you. We're trying to get west. My family. Got caught in Whitehorse. No threat here. Why don't you and yours come in? Break bread with us."

The night is stuck in some in-between hour, the light bruised and dark. Before there would have been crickets in the bushes, but now there are neither bushes nor crickets. A line of sweat looses behind Ben's ear. It feels like a tiny bug making its way through his hair. He lowers the gun and forces himself to breathe. Everything is invisible in the white.

MARANDA

She finds herself inside, at a foldout table, and moves her fingers over the surface. Rough divots, plastic. Last she remembers she was in a car, but a hole's been snipped in her memory. Did she fall asleep?

There're people all around. People she doesn't know. She can feel their bodies. She has to fight not to freak the fuck out.

You're okay. You're okay, a calm voice says. Guardian.

She looks around without trying to look like she's looking around. She's in a camper, which makes her immediately claustrophobic, but she swallows the feeling, wiggles her feet. She's dressed and can move her arms and legs. That's good, better than sometimes. The bottoms of her jeans are cuffed with mud.

Ben's here too. In the kitchen nearby. He's talking to another guy, who's maybe in his sixties. He's got a beard and stringy hair, wearing a paper medical mask.

As she looks at Ben, all she can think about is that *he paid for it.* She thought she'd escaped from those years in the life, and now Ben's just another john. You can't get away from it, can you? For a while she thought she would vomit, wondering what he was like, if as a trick he was pushy or a bitch or one of the creeps that wanted you to think they loved you, but now she honestly doesn't care.

People don't change, especially people like Ben. Maybe he thinks he can fool her, use her. Whatever. *Why's* not her business. He's nothing to her now, not her husband, just a man like any other. They'll get to Anchorage and that will be that.

"I'm telling you," the other man is saying, swiveling his head to include her. "I never felt anything like that. It was like you were all opened up, and I punched you right in the heart."

He taps Ben on the chest and mimes being breathless, eyes boggled.

Looks like he's gonna blow a load, Klara says.

Maranda flinches, closes her eyes. Shut up.

Still, it makes her look at the guy twice. Study him for cracks. You see all sorts in the life. Teachers, officers, pastors, lawyers. Everyone's got to eat, don't they? And it's easy to tell if a guy's hungry or not. There's like a proto-sensor in her gut. There was that guy in her old apartment complex, before she moved in with Ben. The aura he had. Never made a pass, never leered, but every time she looked there were red tendrils curling off his face. Ben told her she was nuts, but within the year they got the guy for kiddy porn.

"Shit," the old guy says, tapping a spoon on the rim of a pot. "Just…shit."

He scoops a portion onto a paper plate and hands it to her. Then another to an even older woman and another to maybe his daughter, a woman about Maranda's own age. There's another man in a plaid hat and Carhartt's standing against the wall. They're all wearing those paper blue medical masks. The younger guy has his pulled beneath his nose. He looks away when Maranda notices him and gets his own plate.

"Spoons, Dad," the daughter says.

"I thought maybe they dropped the bomb, you know," Ben says.

The older man snaps, pointing at the Carhartt's guy.

"Said the same thing," Carhartt's says. "They still aren't saying what it was. Sure as hell felt like that though. Damn."

The older man grabs a fistful of plastic spoons from a box and smushes them onto the table. It startles her, and for a moment all she can hear is an internal cacophony. She has to close her eyes until the voices quiet and she can get back beneath her own feet.

On her plate is a mound of rice and beans still in the shape of the scoop. They've eaten nothing but energy bars and cans of tuna for forever now, and when she takes a bite heat blooms in her chest. It's glorious. It occurs to her that maybe anyone other than Ben would have been able to get them something consistently hot to eat. Just another thing she's apparently not worth.

She can feel herself getting fired up, some of the others too, so she takes a breath and tries to get a wooden spoon across the feeling. Not for Ben's sake, but because if she lets herself go out any further it's going to be a while before she can pull it back.

The daughter has taken one of the spoons and is feeding the old woman, who's just *gone*, you can tell. The daughter pulls the mask under her chin and pushes a bite—a bean, a few grains of rice—but the old bird barely opens her lips.

Maranda must be staring, because the daughter says, "She was like this before."

The kitchen is directly behind the driver's cab. On her other side is a living area, where there's a faux-leather couch and behind that a surprisingly long bay of sleeping compartments. The floor is crowded with trash bags and duffels. There's a wall clock against a stack of books.

Ben's still talking to the old guy and his son, but when he finally gets his plate he looks down, pausing, and closes his eyes. Maranda all but double-takes.

It flashes into her mind, clear as a knife, Louise, Luke, all the wifeys sitting at a dingy table. A casserole Louise will later hold against them. Louise says they're a family, and Maranda believes it. She has them clasp their hands and thank god for their blessings. When they're done eating Louise cleans up and Luke takes them out to the track.

Suddenly, it's like she's looking through the wrong end of binoculars. Her field of vision has a border. Everything hurts, knee to belly button. She's a lever with a present end and a past end. Right now someone's tilted up the present side, and she's sliding back into the past.

In her head Axel says: *Slow up, bitch.*

Okay, she thinks. She tries to focus. Breathe. Breathe, breathe.

The old man's voice is watery, like he needs to cough but won't. "Russia's getting pushy," he says. "Korea too. You folks keep up with the news?"

"Not much," Ben says.

"Don't blame you. Big aftershock yesterday. Killed a whole bunch of people up in, uh, Fairbanks I think."

"Really?"

Maranda focuses. The daughter is spooning individual grains of rice into her grandmother's mouth but the old lady just stares at the wall.

"Whole bunch, yeah." The old man takes a bite and keeps talking. "Not many people to be seen out here." He nods at Ben. "Might be good to, uh, you know, stick together."

Things begin to slow down. It's a proposition, she realizes.

Too many thoughts crowd together. Anxieties and possibilities all at once. The grandmother's head is tilted. Maranda can feel the Carhartt's guy looking up and down her back. She tries to breathe slowly. Ben nods at the older man, and then looks across the camper to Maranda and as soon as he does she feels the other guy's eyes move away. The younger woman, still feeding her grandmother, glances at Ben. She tucks a strand of hair behind her ear.

Again, things start to slide. Maranda presses at her right eye and shakes her head. She hears the sound of rocks scraping down an internal board.

Inside, it feels like a flower blooming up. Like someone else is suddenly bodied, filling her skin like water in a balloon. She feels Klara reaching out through the end of her arms, moving her fingers, her back. Even her mind stretches and groans as Klara's thoughts squeeze out her own.

The younger man has not stopped looking since they came in.

Ben coughs into his fist and says to the old man, "Hey, I never got your name."

The old man wipes his hand on the back of his legs and holds it out. "August Farnsworth. This is my daughter, Penelope. And David, my son. That's my mother. She's…" There is a space where they are all waiting for August to continue but he doesn't.

David's eyes are fingering her spine. She feels it all the way to her calves.

"Pleasure," Ben says. He clears his throat. "I'm Ben. Watters. This is my…"

"Klara," she hears herself say, quickly, sliding a knife into the conversation.

Maranda directs a thought at Klara: *Bitch.*

But Klara laughs. *It is a good plan,* she says. *Smart. Now they all think we speak with an accent.*

David is looking with even more hunger. Part of her is repulsed by this, but the Klara part experiences a jolt down her spine, to her feet, rooting her to Mother Earth. This is the way a man *should* look at a woman.

David says, "That's quite the accent you've got, Klara. You from Toronto?"

"Sweden."

"Is that right?"

Everything's telescoping. She watches as Klara produces a tube of lipstick Maranda forgot she even had, and suddenly she feels like not using it more often is such a shame—it does such nice things for her mouth.

You can see the jealousy on Ben's face. She's surprised at how much she sees of him—the desire like a battery in his gut, and how he hates himself for missing that his wife can turn it on when she wants to. But now she does, and he's worried that these men, even the old one, have a better chance of laying her than he does, which only makes him hotter.

She does the lipstick down one side, then the other, slow, looking in Ben's eyes the entire time. It is so good to be seen, to wield something and feel its weight in your hands. She can't tell if this is her thought or Klara's, but it hardly matters. Things are dropping farther and farther away.

BEN

Ben wakes in the middle of the night to the sounds of laughter, muted glasses tinkling. For a moment he thinks he's back in Tennessee, his father still at the table with one of the deacons or their neighbor Vernon, drinking and theologizing. Ben would wake in the small hours to shouting matches about end times, predestination, whatever. The man never had more than a single drink, but his anger, he liked to say, was always for a righteous cause. To Ben, the hand of God was his father's fist, calloused, still with its silver wedding band, smacking the kitchen table in cadence, cups and cutlery shivering.

He shakes his head. Blue blankets, chromed walls. The bed next to him is empty, but the sheets are warm. From the living area, he hears the tail of a whispered conversation, laughter. A deep voice says the word *natural.*

He inches the curtain aside. His wife is sitting on the vinyl couch holding a drink. She's in one of his oxfords with a lit cigarette between her middle and index fingers. He watches as she unfolds her legs to cross them the other way. David's arm is on the back of the couch, behind her.

Well, not exactly his wife. His wife who is not his wife. He'd first met Klara one night when he and Maranda had been fighting and she'd already had two gins, finishing a third. It had looked like she was falling asleep in the middle of their argument—a relief to Ben, an excuse to be angry, since the whole thing had been about him not calling when he was going to be late from a trip, but he hadn't been late at all, stopping at a hotel on the way home, figuring she would buy the excuse—but then all of a sudden Maranda was fully awake again, looking at the drink in her hand with distaste, and asked if perhaps there was…*vodka*?

They'd fucked that night, Klara's idea, and from then on he recognized the hunger that occasionally came into his wife's eyes in the middle of sex. It wasn't a second wind or sudden desire, it was Klara. He did a few Google searches, suspected there were more personalities hidden away, but things were already falling apart, so it seemed easier not to find out any more.

Ben lets the curtain back. He can hear her laughing. "That is not okay," she says. "Goodness. You say this? Really?"

"Well," David says. "You know. What are you gonna do?"

Ben closes his eyes. He feels a throbbing behind his navel. Doesn't know exactly what it is but can tell it's nothing good. When he looks out again Klara is tracing her toe against David's leg.

She says, "Why don't we, eh, go outside?"

David doesn't say anything, but the camper shifts. A moment later the door screes open, then shuts.

Ben tips his head back. He takes air into his lungs and holds it until his chest burns.

"The hell," he says, and scooches up on the bed.

The two of them are moving like ghosts away from the camper. Klara leads David by the hand. They stop a ways out, past the circle of glow, under the cover of the trees. He watches her kneel and touch his belt.

Ben sinks back. For a moment he can hear David talking, a canned indistinct sound, but then they aren't talking anymore. Ben's mind goes unmoored from his body. The light in the compartment is a dead blue. They aren't talking anymore. He doesn't watch, though a part of him wants to, or masturbate, though a part of him wants to do that too. He isn't proud of it, but he's not exactly ashamed either. It's like a ritual he has to endure, that he deserves. He thinks, weirdly, that maybe the score between them, while not even, is now tipped more toward balanced than it was in the morning.

Out there he can hear the sound of another man, low and animalistic, and the sound of his wife who is not his wife. Everything goes out of him, his arms like so much dead weight. His penis just impotent flesh. And as he sits there and listens it feels like he's not there at all. He hears a sound from her, a moan he has never listened closely to before, and though it is Klara he still knows it to be Mar, still recognizes the sound, and it brings him out of himself and into a present that he can't ignore, however much he may want to.

He's outside in three steps, the camper door bonging open springlessly. He moves through a purple dark—never night or day anymore—and around to the back. Ben wants to look and he wants to avert his eyes. David swears, starts struggling his pants up. Klara purses her lips and backs away smirking.

There's a sunflare in Ben's belly. His heart's a bloody fist. He wants to take her here, now, but then he's half-ill too. He's a dozen different things. He's fury, he's sex. He's humiliation and rage. As he moves across the clearing things slow down. He can spin them around and rotate them in his mind. David bending at the waist, chin against his chest. He's trying to fumble his belt together as he brings his pants up. Klara keeps smoothing out her shirt. The sky is a smear of bruise. The trees all look like men who've been shot but don't realize they're dead.

"Uh, hey," David grunts.

Ben recognizes the knot in his voice. The block when you try to force normal. He's used this voice. Ben's on him in two strides. David still has his face down, waist-level. Ben plants his right foot and place-kicks, a hand out for balance. It feels good. The muscle is tight and strong all the way up his hamstring into his ass.

David snaps backward, his body loose, flailing. There's immediate blood. At any other time the movement might be funny, Ben thinks.

"…the fuck?"

Ben steps back, brings his hands up and swings sloppy-but-hard, landing in the soft spot between David's ear and neck. He feels something cartilage-y crunch and David's face contorts. His head jerks down toward the blow.

"What the hell, man?"

Ben says nothing. It feels like he's stepped naturally into this, having barely been a part of what could be considered a fight before. Turns out there'd been a space at the table waiting. He thinks about his limbs, his mind, his muscles, tries to make everything happen the way he wants it to.

He's been imitating Sylvester Stallone, bouncing on his feet and shaking out his neck. He realizes this and feels ridiculous, but not enough to stop. He wants Maranda—or Klara or *any* of them, really—to be watching. Out the corner of his eye, he can see her shaking her head, pressing at one eye as she stumbles for the camper. A little globe of vindication—like a bath bomb—releases in his gut, but along with it a surge of pity. He wonders if Maranda even knows what happened.

David is leaning with his elbows on his thighs. He touches his ear, looks at his hand.

"Listen," Ben starts.

But no sooner does he say it than David charges into Ben with a sloppy form-tackle. All the air goes out. Ben goes backward a few steps before he can get his feet under him, then he grabs David by the arms and tries to lean him into the ground. They stomp through a firepit and when Ben looks down David lets go, and before Ben can duck or anything there's a blank space and he's sitting on the ground.

It feels like he's wearing half a mask over the left side of his face. He can tell David got in a solid punch, though he doesn't remember it.

The sun is making spokes of fire in the trees. There are no birds anywhere.

Ben shakes his head. He can't think. He touches the ground, tries to move smoothly from sitting to kneeling like this is just a casual thing but he can't get his legs to do what he's telling them. He slumps, hands folded in his lap. He can't think. He shakes his head but it won't clear.

For a moment there are two Davids touching their necks, looking at their fingers and wiping them on their pants. Then only one.

"She came onto *me* anyway," he says. "Jesus."

Ben's eye is already swollen. He doesn't touch it. There's pressure, a strange bulk, when he blinks. He can see his nose in his field of vision.

Finally, he's able to stagger-walk his way to the camper, where what looks to be his wife is standing frozen, staring at nothing. He touches her elbow and she flinches.

"What the hell?" she says when she notices his face. It sounds, maybe, like genuine concern.

"Is this—" He feels like he has to sit. "Is this you?"

"What?"

"Is it you?" The words, rushed and loud, spook her.

He has to sit down, does. A door slams. He hears people moving and yelling in the camper. The engine turns over, and it pulls onto the road and heads west. Soon all you can see of it are lights in the mist, then even the lights are gone and you can only hear the rolling *pbtpbt* of the engine. Then silence.

MARANDA

Standing in the middle of the road as the camper disappears into the fog, Maranda spikes what's left of a water bottle to the ground.

Mr. Savior-Man. Mr. Goddamn Hero.

She's got no idea what the hell is going on, but their one lifeline has just disappeared because Ben had to start something and then get his ass kicked.

"Well, any idea how to get back to Route 1?" she bites. "Cause I sure as hell don't."

"It's not far," Ben mutters. "There's a junction."

He's watching her over the top of the car. The swelling has moved into his forehead, his nose. It looks like shit.

"What?" she says.

"I saw."

"You *what?*"

"I saw. You and David."

He's lying. The cheating motherfucker is trying to lie again. He's selfish as hell and lies like a nine-year-old. Once she found porn in his browser history and he told her he'd been investigating their antivirus software. Seriously. He used those exact words.

But even as she thinks this, she can tell what's happening now is different. Beneath her feet is a vacuum. She stays on the anger-tightrope, refusing to look down.

The truth is, the last thing she remembers is sitting at a fold-out table, the daughter noticing Ben, the balance of things starting to slide away. That was Klara coming out. Then it's all blank until morning. But Ben *has* to be lying. To consider that something may actually have happened would be to acknowledge a reality far more blind and terrifying, the mute horror around which she has always revolved.

"I don't know what you're talking about."

He makes a kind of mirthless snort. She knows damn well what he's talking about, but you never hand your unarmed accuser a weapon.

Anyway, ironic, right? *She's* not the cheater.

Wind moves in the branches. Somewhere, distant fire is grinding the forest between its teeth. She opens the passenger door and gets in.

He's always had this ego. Little man syndrome or something. He'd come home from work and bitch about what this person had said, or what he'd quipped back to so-and-so. You eventually had to stop paying attention. It was incredible, literally incredible—as in, so extreme as to not be believable—how readily Ben could flip a problem around until it was a direct reflection of his masculinity.

He gets in the car and adjusts his crotch. Makes a show of taking deep calming breaths, like he's Gandhi, and leans back and checks for the third time that their stuff is in the back. He starts the ignition and pulls out sharply.

Fucking Ben—subjecting yourself to actual physical intercourse with him—was nightmarishly convoluted. He was eager and experimental and he held back and all that, but after a while you started to realize it was only because he felt good and masculine and strong making you come. It was some kind of masturbatory boost for him. All the things he did weren't for you, they were for him. Like he was having sex with himself, and you were the proxy.

"Maybe we should ask Klara," he finally says.

"Maybe we should," she says. "*I* don't remember anything."

"That makes me feel a lot better. You know, like, how am I supposed to feel about that?"

Maranda tongues the inside of her mouth. "Mm, I don't know. I don't know how *I* feel about it. But given that you, I don't know, fucked a hooker, you think you might be—"

"No, you know what, this is a serious problem, regardless of me. They're putting you in danger. Klara lost your phone. She's trying to screw other guys, which is bad enough, but what if that ended worse? What if David decided he wanted to get violent with *you* instead of me? They—" he points a finger at her head and makes a circling motion. "*They* can't be out of control like that."

It's the way he says *they*. A tone you'd use for cockroaches.

Inside, someone is laughing.

What if he's right? What if Klara *did* fuck that guy? She remembers the gas station—the guy's tongue on his teeth— and wants to be sick.

Maranda shakes her head, rolling it out both ways. The hum of tires on pavement. She feels Ben glance at her, hears him start to say, "Hey, no," but a plug has already been pulled. She's draining.

BEN

He knows a change by its beginning now. Can just tell.

He says her name a few times, but she doesn't hear. Her eyes are far off, staring through things.

Honestly, he doesn't like being around when she switches. Dread seeps into his gut every time. He doesn't understand the half of it, but there's something uncontainable about the process. He can't bring himself to even attempt to imagine what could have happened that would shatter a person in such a way.

After Axel, part of it's just plain fear—you can't predict what form she'll take, or what they'll do once they're out. It's like standing on a subway platform as lights wash down the tunnel. You can tell a train is coming, but until it actually pulls up you don't know which one.

This one, it seems, is Chipmunk. The older ones need a moment to stretch out their new skin, but Chipmunk just blinks, looks around, and smiles, immediately at home.

She leans forward in her seat, trying to get his attention, sitting up and bending *way* over into his field of vision. It looks ridiculous, and he tries to pull his face tight, not smile—because *of course* this has to happen right in the middle of him actually having a legitimate issue to address— and just as he starts to fail she catches sight of something and *thunks* her forehead against the window.

"Look!" she cries, her fingers pressed to the glass like gecko pads. She turns her head to follow a half-leveled playground as they pass.

Ben glances at the mirror. "Yeah," he says.

"Can we?"

For Christ's sake. He's not a babysitter. She just messed around with a guy. How is he supposed to deal with this?

"No," he says, quickly. "No."

Her face might be shattered glass for how it falls.

The whole thing's overly convenient, right? He's angry at Maranda—technically Klara—but then there's only Chipmunk—a *six-year-old*—to talk to. What is he even supposed to say?

He tries not to look at her, but he can see her jut out her lower lip into an exaggerated pout. Ben shakes his head. "Look, come on. You guys can't be out doing all this stuff, right? What am I supposed to do?"

She's still pouting, but her forehead knits into half-anger now too.

"You guys can't take over," he continues. "It's not fair."

Chipmunk scoots up. She looks right at him. "I don't know what Klara did, but I just want to play. That's not fair too. *I* didn't do anything." She sits back and crosses her arms.

The day is still shrouded in white. He can almost make out a shapeless, limpid sun. Like it's looking in on Earth from the outside, waiting to see what they'll do.

Ben glances at Chipmunk. Her hands are pressed between her knees.

"Fine," he sighs. "Fine."

He pulls the car over the rumble strips and starts to turn around. If one of them is crazy it's very likely him.

He'd felt similarly nuts when he asked Maranda out the second time, finding himself a few nights later back at the banquet hall. He was pretty sure she'd say no, after all they hadn't exchanged numbers, names, anything, just done it and then done it again and when he woke in the morning she was gone. He'd hooked up plenty and had once in a while, you know, hired a girl, but he had the sense Maranda wasn't even trying. She had sex the way she served tables— like she could do in her sleep what other people had to bust their asses for.

He'd arrived late, after a shift, trying to be casual about it, and asked if maybe she wanted to get a drink and she'd blinked and said sure, and that was it. She was so deadpan and he was so surprised she'd actually said yes that he'd begun to wonder if maybe he'd asked the wrong girl. But it *was* her, of course. Wasn't it?

Chipmunk runs ahead into the empty lot. Ben follows, hands in his pockets.

All around them are dead trees. The playground is little more than a ghost. Swings creaking in the no-wind. Chipmunk is touching the bar of a roundabout, the metal bare but for the rust and a few stubborn splotches of red.

She scrambles on, then lifts her eyebrows at Ben.

The metal scrapes and sings as he gives the thing a heave. Chipmunk holds her legs and when he turns it faster she shoots out a hand to clutch a post and snorts.

He remembers a day, maybe a Saturday, not long before they were married. They'd gone to Mendenhall and even though it was chilly they drove with their windows down, eating up miles of wilderness, the air a bracing rudeness that filled the car. She'd just cut her hair short and couldn't stop touching it. He kept telling her he loved it and, truthfully, he did.

At some point, Ben had put his hand out the window and reached over the top of the car, making a puppet with his hand. He'd started babbling nonsense, doing what he imagined to be an impression of the adults in *Peanuts* but he knew sounded only ridiculous. It made her laugh though, so he kept at it.

She was so often sad without explanation. She would all of a sudden lapse into anger or tears or she would lash out at him and it was work for him to be able to follow her line of thinking. He'd thought then that there was a connection between laughter and happiness, between happiness and health, and so he'd done whatever he could to be funny, even though he wasn't, not really, a funny person. He used to think he could save her, he's realizing, and when that didn't happen he alternated between blaming himself and blaming her.

But in this memory, in the car, she's laughing. She's throwing her head back and he feels like a king. She stretches her arm from the window and stands on her knees and does her own voice and they puppet-talk back and forth over the top of the car, the cold like silk all around them.

Nothing feels like that anymore. Not now. The sky is dark and Halloweenishly tinged, sliced with ribbons that might be smoke, might be fallout, might be literally-God-only-knows-what, and Maranda is a six-year-old climbing a shitty rest stop slide.

Chipmunk has her tongue between her teeth, focusing on where she puts her hands and feet. Ben feels the need to safeguard, not quite touching her legs because that, somehow, feels inappropriate. The chute's only a foot or two longer than she is, but she comes down squealing, hands up and one foot over the edge. When Ben helps her up, she stands and embraces him.

"I never get to play," she says.

All his frustration drops away like old skin. He coughs, hesitantly hugging her back.

"Can I swing?" she asks, pivoting a toe in the dirt.

The swing-set's mostly shit, just two regular seats and an infant one, the rubber all cracked and gray. He makes her wait while he cleans off a dusting of ash with his sleeve.

He's being rendered, he can tell. Day by day, there's less of what had once been him. He can feel it falling from his bones. When she caught him, and when they first set out, he'd been like an animal caught by the tail, thrashing itself wild. It's only now, days later, that he's starting to settle into a kind of exhaustion that feels almost peaceful.

Maybe he's spending too much time trying to figure all this out. Trying to define Chipmunk, her relationship to him, whether she's part of his wife or a sickness or a shard that's broken off. She's just Chipmunk, maybe. That's enough.

The chains of the swing are squeaking and Chipmunk, midair, throws her head back and laughs. He can hear the wind and the fire somewhere far off, but it's distant enough, he's pretty sure. They've got time. He catches the seat and pulls it back until she's facing the ground.

"Ready?" he says.

"Uh-huh."

"*Ready?*"

His voice echoes. When she yells "yes" again, he runs forward, throwing her out ahead of him and sprinting underneath. She swings upward, yowling, and the sound of real, actual joy is a startling blast of color against the trees, against what he's always thought of as his life.

There's a bulldozer parked beside a wooden sign on which is stenciled WELCOME TO BEAVER CREEK. Not much to the place but a few lodges, a gas station with a fallen roof, and a municipal border building. There's gray and silty water hushing over gravel.

In the lot behind the gas station is a large fire surrounded by about ten people. Men, women, children. There are cars behind them in a watching circle.

The Pilot stops on the shoulder. The younger, scratchy guy gets out and rolls his neck while the driver shrugs his jacket on and opens a toolbox in the back. He carefully pockets something. Together they walk toward the fire, their boots loud on the stones.

"Evening folks," the blazered man calls.

A man in coveralls and a baseball hat separates himself from the group. Another man does the same, this one smaller and wearing a sweatshirt for some now-irrelevant fundraiser. They all shake hands.

"What can we help you with?" the first guy says.

He scans the faces at the fire. A few of them glance and whisper. They're all dark-eyed and tired, but none of them are Maranda.

"You all haven't seen a silver car pass this way, have you? Would've been," he turns to his partner, "what?"

"Few hours ago."

"Three, four hours ago, maybe."

The men look at each other. "I don't think so," the smaller one says.

"Huh."

There's only one other adult male. A teenage girl watches from the far side, her features watery through the flame. The blazered man lingers, holding eye contact.

The smaller guy continues. "Few cars gone by, but I didn't notice the colors, you know."

"See it's…it's important."

The first man coughs into a fist. "No, yeah I bet. Who's, uh, who is it?"

"It's his…" the blazered man jerks his head. "His cousin."

"My sister," his partner says at the same time.

The two men look like they were hoping this would turn out to be a joke but the moment drags on and it doesn't.

"Oh," the first one says.

The blue-blazered man holds up his left hand. He raises three fingers for the men to see. His partner looks too, for effect. Ringed by the neck between his thumb and middle finger is a brown field mouse that is very much alive, pushing at his fingers with its feet.

"Sure you can't tell us anything? Brother?"

The men look at the mouse and then at each other and then at him.

"I'm sorry?" the second one says. He gives a small laugh.

The blazered man raises his other hand and pinches the tail with his thumb and index finger. He does it with a flourish, like a showman, and snaps. The men both flinch, and the mouse starts writhing, the tail alive in his other hand, snake-like, coiling and uncoiling from his fingers.

"Hey now…" the second guy says, stepping backward. "We don't want—"

He drops the tail. "No? Nothing?" Quickly, he does the same to a leg. The mouse makes a terrible, high-pitched noise that is so constant it sounds almost digital. The first guy covers his mouth. Near the fire, the group murmurs, shuffling.

"Jesus."

He pulls another leg. The mouse continues to scream. Another. There are runnels of blood down his hand and wrist.

The two men are now openly backing away. The first one has his hands up. The other crouches down and regurgitates a spatter of yellow.

He spikes what's left of it. "Okay then."

His partner pulls a gun. Someone screams. The smaller man grabs his companion, vomit still on his face, and pulls him away but then he vomits too. His partner fires into the air, the flash illuminating his arm, his laughing face while the jacketed man stalks toward the fire. A few people run to their cars and others make for the burned grass by the lake. Someone splashes in. The teenaged girl is standing there crying until she sees him and then she tries to run but it's too late. She swings at him and he catches it. He doesn't even hit her, just drags her to the Pilot. She's screaming now and his partner is waiting with the gun for someone to come after them but no one does.

MARANDA

Honestly, she's hardly sure who she is anymore. If this is her or one of the voices filtering from underneath, but as they drive, it feels good to be moving. To have the motion of the car in your body. If only Ben would speed a little. He's only going, what, eighty kilometers per hour, which is well under the speed limit.

Wait. Who the hell thinks in kilometers?

It's got to be someone else. Klara, probably.

Great.

When she pulls down the mirror, it doesn't look like her face. She finds herself thinking, *Maranda's body. Maranda's hair. Maranda's face.*

What if Klara *did* screw that guy? And if so, have there been others? It's a strange feeling. She doesn't feel guilty, exactly, because it's not strictly *her,* but at the same time it feels like she ought to scrub herself raw.

She's had just about enough of never being in control. As a kid, with Louise, and now *them*—the voices. She wants to be the one calling the goddamn shots. But she doesn't even know how to begin.

Hey, she thinks. She does her best to direct her thoughts inward, as firmly as possible. *You guys can't do that. Klara, you can't screw somebody else.*

She can hear some of them, deeper inside, agreeing, but Klara's not having it.

The man at the camper, Klara says, *I do not love him. But we are physical creatures with physical desires. If a man wants to eat a meal I want to serve, why can't I do this and walk away?*

You just can't, Maranda thinks. *I don't want to be the person who does that. And if I decide something, that's the way it has to go. You can't.*

Klara flips the mirror back up, sighs.

The world dissolves around them. Ben has the radio on. A reporter says, "*The US announced their intention for full-scale…any anticipated terrorist attacks.*"

Alongside the road, there's a powder gray river of sludge. There's wood and waste in the water, an entire house. A whole entire house floats down the water. Beyond, fires crinkle and spread across the lower parts of the mountain. It feels like a dream.

"*In other reports, the number of refugees in Anchorage is threatening to overwhelm relief efforts. Authorities fear rioting. Yesterday, a group attempted…control of an airplane. Three people were killed, including a police officer. Another four were wounded.*"

This whole time, Ben has said not one thing. She expected him to be angrier. Like Luke. But Ben has never hit, has he? He's never hit.

It is getting hard to focus. She closes her eyes. When she opens them again, they are driving through the leftovers of a forest. Nothing moves. Ben is only watching the road, only driving, and he seems mostly gone. She's surprised to find she misses him.

Okay, Klara says to Maranda, and her voice is softer now. *Okay.*

The woman on the radio says: *"Whatever cataclysm struck the Yukon, its implications have been unquestionably global, and dire. This reporter hopes for—"* and then cuts off, out of contact. The volume had been up very loud, and the loudness of the static punches her from every side. For a moment all that noise fills the car, and she can hear nothing else, not even her thoughts. It is welcoming and warm until Ben turns it off.

She's got no idea how she and Ben even started dating. He just showed up one day and asked her out. It terrified her, but it was weirdly fairy-tale too. He didn't even know her name, but he wanted to take her out. Outside of the life, he was the first person to show any interest. Of course then, yeah, maybe he could help her get south, protect her, but if she's being honest, having someone want her was the draw. Like maybe if someone wanted her, she could stop running from her mind's devouring storm.

She stares out the window, her face near-transparent. An ugly face, she thinks, and tries not to look so hard.

They drive past shacks and lodges. All of them collapsed or slanted to one side, like someone blew on a house of cards—*poof*—and that was it.

She's scared. Everyone's scared. Even Mother Earth is scared—you can feel her trembling. She can feel the beat of her own blood.

They pass an old bulldozer perimetered with weeds. Beside it is a crooked sign that reads WELCOME TO BEAVER CREEK.

Ben pulls into a loose gravel lot between a ruined gas station and a lodge with a sign about RV Hookups. He leaves the door open and motions at the store.

"I need to stretch my legs," he says. "Then let's check that out."

But as she steps outside, something opens in her belly. A hunted feeling. In the space of a moment she's already flood-full of panic.

Come on, she hears Axel say. *Don't piss around right now.*

And then Guardian says, *Wait.* It's strong and toneless. Not a command, an announcement. This is what's going to happen. We're going to *Wait.*

There are no cars here. You can smell the wind coming off the lake. Rot and water and smoke all together. Guardian moves into the forefront of her mind and starts scanning the environment. The lodge is mostly intact, a single wall missing. Farther down, the gas station's canopy is entirely canted over to its side.

A thousand beetles are under her skin. She's going to explode if she sits here any longer. At least *move,* she thinks. At least get out and move.

She shuts the door behind her. Looks around. The trees are limbed with clouds. The sky so close it's physical. Something's coming. As certain as she's ever been of anything, something's coming.

Halfway across the lot, she notices a brown puff in the gravel. She takes a few steps, kneels, and is almost touching it when everything crashes. As soon as she sees what it is—a brown field mouse, legless—her brain hits a brick wall doing ninety. The world goes slow-motion. The inside of her head is instantaneously bulleted with knives and glass.

She knows who did this.

There's a flashback quivering at the border of her mind. A girl sobbing, Luke, sitting on the edge of her bed, holding a rabbit by the legs.

He says, "I'll stop as soon as you say yes."

She tries to smooth tears from her face. Doesn't offer to touch him or let him touch her, but says, "Yes, yes." She says it again, "Yes." Then everything goes dark.

BEN

It's silent out here. No wildlife, no bugs. Just entirely vacated space.

Maranda's crouching in the gravel, cracking her neck. The start of a switch. When she stands up—straight, tall—he can tell right away who it is.

Guardian puts on a pair of glasses, then turns and motions Ben closer, holding out a hand. Ben leans in. It's a dismembered mouse, just a head and body. Three of the legs are popped off at the joint, the other one has a little bit of shoulder missing.

"What the hell?"

Guardian drops the thing and brushes a hand on Maranda's thigh. "I know who was shooting at us, back in Juneau. They must still be after us."

Ben's stomach drops. He remembers the phone call, the bemused chuckle at the other end. "Who?"

"This is half a day old, maybe. Maybe less. They must have passed us when we were with the Farnsworths."

Ben can feel the heartbeat in his neck. "Who? Guardian, who's following us?"

Guardian stoops, taking a long look at the mouse and sighing. "That's Maranda's tale to tell, Ben."

Guardian drives them out of Beaver Creek. The sky's reflection washes over the windshield. The car rattles, and half the rear windshield's blown out. It's so easy for a thing to fall apart.

After a while Maranda switches back in. At least it seems like it's her.

She'd always talked about going south. That was her plan. They'd hooked up in December, she moved into his place that April, and they got married in June. The whole time she talked about wanting to head for the Lower 48, but he figured she was like the others who couldn't crack it up here. Not that she was running from something.

She's fog to him. A bridge over which he can't see the other side. He can't even keep track of her. She keeps squawking at him from different branches, but when he gets there she doesn't want to be caught. How long before you give up, if that's what she's bent on? She wants openness, but she doesn't tell him anything about herself. She might as well have not existed before two years ago, that's how little he knows. No family, no friends. Here they are, in the middle of a disaster, and she can't tell him *anything*?

He knows it's hypocritical, but still.

He sits up, clears his throat. "Who's in Anchorage?"

She doesn't answer.

"Mar. What happened?"

There are tears in her eyes. Slowly, he touches her arm, expecting her to flinch, but she doesn't. The sun freckles the car as they pass underneath what's left of the trees.

They crest a pass in the Uplands. Below are patches of stubbornly green forest, no order or reason at all. The day is clear around them, at least as clear as days get now, but farther off a black hand presses the sky low.

In the middle distance, three tornados gyre and lumber and turn on themselves, almost but never quite touching the ground.

In the evening, he pulls them off at a wooden campground, hidden down a pot-holed lane. Trees and brush all filmy with ash. There's a flat area overlooking a lake. A few RV hookups—all dead.

Ben sits at a picnic table, his hands tented against his mouth. Stream rises from the water. It looks like something ancient and alive, like it might at any moment yield a monster.

He's left the radio on, the doors open and the car running.

"Today, the largest earthquake in recorded history hit Santiago. Measuring in at just over 11 on the Richter scale, aftershocks were said to be felt as far north as Texas. Tsunamis have…survivors expected to be minimal."

There's a long pause. Finally the reporter continues.

"Some groups are speculating on the cosmic, even divine origins of these events."

Ben's already thinking it. Every hour things are sliding more and more to hell. Whatever comes, there's no going back to the way things were.

His eyes go up from the lake. The sky ripples pink and brown above the trees. It's too much, he thinks. Do you think I can do this by myself? Because I can't.

He drops his head. Hell. He doesn't even know who he's talking to.

The reporter says: *"Regardless, worldwide, the crises that started last week in the Yukon seem to be escalating…"* and then the car shuts off.

Maranda emerges, straightening her jacket and holding the keys. She walks up and sits on the bench behind him, pulling nervously at her fingers.

"Sure *sounds* like people think it's the end of the world," he fake-laughs. "I mean—"

"Growing up," she interrupts, "my father would rape me."

She says it the way you would say, *Growing up, we rode our bikes to school.* The words vibrate like a struck bell.

Ben opens his mouth, then closes it.

"Eventually I ran away. After a few days a lady picked me up and gave me a place to stay. She told me I was special, and I'd never heard that before. Not once. And it was the nicest bed I've ever slept in. Like, seriously. Ever. Before or after."

Steam lifts into the sky like upside-down rain. Ben realizes he knows what she's going to say before she even says it. That, somehow, he's known for a while now.

"The next night she introduced me to a guy. Luke. He did the thing with the legs. The mouse. He used to…I thought he was my boyfriend, but he was, whatever. You know. I spent the next seven years…getting sold, Ben. Me and other girls. I wasn't old enough to drive when I started."

He looks at her, but she's far away. She blows into her hands even though the night is close and warm.

"Luke's the guy shooting at us, I think. I don't know how he found me."

She could be a stranger right now. Is a stranger. He has no idea what to say. Things are falling out from underneath him. No, from *inside* him. What do you say? He's going to vomit. The whole world is being sucked down a hole, and it's trying to pull him down too, down into a place from which he'll never, ever be able to crawl back.

MARANDA

The whole time she's talking she can barely feel herself. No, not true. She can *too strongly* feel herself. Feels blood ventricling through her chest, into her neck, barely constrained from arcing out in a mad spray.

She's barely there, she's too much there—story of her life.

Her memory's shot full of holes, machine-gunned to flimsy. She's stringing it together as best she can, but to be honest her goal isn't narrative right now, and it sure as hell isn't about Ben. What she wants is to get this out of her, and Ben's here, isn't he? He's here. The best she can hope for is that all of this will leave her and float off, smaller and smaller, up into a sky that looks bent on devouring everything anyway.

She means to tell him about her teenage years, the first part of her twenties, but what comes to mind right away is *IT*. Her father sprawled amid a dozen beer cans on a stained couch, watching underwater, fleshy things on the TV.

No. Not that. She's not ready for that.

Pain is already peeking over the horizon. Just as it grows to the point where she can tell it's going to be the kind that overcomes her, she feels herself borne away, and it recedes. Hands lift and carry her off. Just by the feel, she knows it's Guardian and a few of the others, pulling her back from the edge.

She breathes. Thinks, *thank you.*

After that, memories go past in a shredded-up scroll. She sees a townhouse, paintings on the wall. Her own self fourteen-years-old and she thinks: *Okay, this. Tell him this.*

Even now, she'd do anything for a crumb from Louise's table. Louise picked Maranda up in the middle of the night, and it was the first meal anyone had offered her for years, even if it was only salad and pizza.

"You're special," Louise says. She's wearing pearls and oven mitts. "I can tell."

What else could she do? Even now, today, if somebody actually thought that about her, she'd probably do it all over again.

That night, the bedroom, the bed. Louise says, "I've got this boy," and they do it. Well, *he* does it. So much desire they both might combust.

That's that.

Louise putting lipstick on her, spinning her around so she can see her reflection in a mirror. Luke in the doorway, all smiles, all charm. He kisses her hand. Maranda already so mind-fucked he might be a perfect gentleman.

A few girls in an unfinished basement. Corners of wet. Luke comes down and points at one of them and she comes back ten minutes later, fixing her hair.

A dingy bedroom. She's on the edge of a bed as a trick zips himself and straightens his tie. She's lying there, watching an ant crawl this way, then that.

She steps back and opens her eyes, and *thank god,* she's on the picnic table. Ben has his back to her.

She shakes her head and keeps talking. "I had, you know, abortions and stuff. Then…but there was this girl there, a little girl. Gracie. And it was kind of like…"

The urge to cry overtakes her before she thought it would. She swallows. "She's in Anchorage, Ben. I want to get there before it's too late."

Ben's silent. She waits, barely breathing, conscious of the fact that she just handed him a knife and precise instructions on how to disassemble her.

Finally, he says, "How…how did you get out?"

But that's hers, at least for now. She drums her fingers on the table, saying nothing. It's one thing to hand over pain, another to hand over your still-frangible self-respect. She doesn't trust him not to break it.

"When?" he asks instead.

She breathes. "Not that long. Six months before I met you."

Ben leans back. He looks away. He has his fingers locked over his head.

There's little to be heard in the clearing but the lake washing on the shore. Ben keeps shaking his head, again and again and again.

She's the one to break the quiet. "Say something."

His mouth is open, but he's not getting anything out. "I'm…I'm…*Fuck,* I mean…God. I'm…Are you *serious?* Shit. It's…"

She watches. She's ready for anything.

Yes. You are, Guardian says.

Ben touches his chest a few times. "I mean…"

She'd hoped, maybe even assumed, that he'd lean in and hug her. The sudden desire to be touched and held surprises her, but it's there, goddamnit, and it's strong, but Ben just stands and moves away. Suddenly, she's cold, exposed.

Fine, she thinks.

You're okay, Guardian says.

In her pocket, she goes for the Calico rabbit. It's Chipmunk who wants it, who's maybe even actually doing it, but the fur against her fingers is comforting nonetheless.

Ben paces back and forth. He bends over like he's going to vomit but doesn't. Instead, he stumbles toward the car, ripping at the locked door.

Ass, Klara says, pathetic and sad.

He falls to beating on the steering wheel. The horn goes each time. Finally, he leans his head on his hands. She stops watching.

There are shapes and shadows on the other side of the lake, but she can't make them out clearly. For whatever reason, this is soothing.

In her mind, she says to her voices: *I guess it's just us now.*

The response is quick: *You think it was ever anything else?*

In the night, she sits on the edge of the lake. Sludge-water licks the shore.

She can hear the hesitancy in Ben's footsteps, like *now* he could break her. He sits and wraps his arms around his knees. Then he scoots himself a few inches closer and repeats the same settling in process all over again.

"Listen," he says, but he doesn't get anything more out before dropping his head. A long time passes. Smoke over the moon. Water shushes up the shore.

Finally, he says, "I know sorry doesn't fix anything. But I am. Sorry, I mean. I want to help. Regardless of what you…decide. With us. I want to help you get to Anchorage, to find her."

She's not sure how to feel about that, or if she even believes him, but before she can say anything he clumsies himself even closer and puts an arm over her shoulder. She exhales. The dark lake-wind goes over them like black ink.

BEN

The morning sun is hazy and weak, little more than a brightening shapelessness. Ben moves around the camp, needlessly tidying. He wants to be doing *something*, anything other than sitting with his thoughts.

One of the first things that went through his head last night was wondering how many guys? Intellectually, yeah, there's a difference between a guy you *want* to sleep with and a guy you're paid to sleep with, but still. How many? And—was it ever good? Ever better?

It's a shitty thing to even think. Now, in the clear light of morning, he's thankful that the volume on all that is at least a little bit tamped down.

He checks his phone before remembering it's dead. Not that it would work anyway. He jiggles it around in his hand, then hauls back and chucks the thing out over the lake, watching it arc and disappear into the water with a quiet *thuk*. Something small and light and free unfolds in his chest.

They're not going back to Juneau. He can see that now. Which means he can't go back to the person he was. There's only forward. Anchorage, fire, and the nightmare of her past.

He looks across the camp at Maranda as she stretches to face the day. He can hardly fathom all this. Can't reconcile it with what he thought he knew. As she pushes a rolled blanket into the trunk, a jet screams overhead, like a zipper pulled open in the sky, so fast it's little more than a ripple of sound. She flinches and ducks, and he feels himself soften. She's so easily shattered. So quickly dust. But at the same time, he knows he wouldn't have survived even half of it.

Looking back, he's able to see that neither of them had been healthy enough for anything even resembling a relationship. But shit, they used to have fun. They got drunk and played Monopoly. She found grasshoppers and gave them names. Once in a while they'd order four desserts in place of dinner, and when he took her to a symphony she wept and said it was "perfect," even though she'd never heard of Stravinsky.

In truth, it felt like he needed her, and that scared him. An instinct woke up when he saw her, and he didn't know if he liked that or not. He told people she was the most real, the most honest person he'd ever met, and that was the truth, but he still couldn't understand her. Other women did everything in their power to be warmer, more inviting, but Maranda was a cliff, and she routinely set about sharpening her edges. Not long after they met she chopped off all her hair and dyed it black, like she was *daring* him to find her attractive—and it was breathtaking.

Still though, he continued to stray. He kept separate bank accounts, cash envelopes. He needed *something,* he told himself. If Maranda would ease up a little bit, but even when she did, he kept going.

Paying for sex was never supposed to become a thing that he did. There's no real conscious decision to look back on—it was more like sliding down a muddy slope. He always thought that at some point it would *end.* He never meant to continue past the point where he was cheating *on* someone, even though he has, he realizes, never *not* been cheating on anyone he's ever dated. He's never admitted this to himself before.

In between relationships it was just something to blow off steam, a secret weakness that would allow him be strong in the other areas where he *needed* to be strong, you know? People were depending on him. And then when he was in a relationship, like when he and Maranda started dating, then it was just to keep him going until they were married, and then after that it became only when he was away and it was only lately, the second to last trip, when he didn't really have to go but it had been a rough month at the pharmacy, and she'd been frigid and so constantly on his case that he'd decided to go "hunting" with no intention of actually hunting. While he was there Maranda had been calling him and calling him and he didn't pick up until after he'd washed himself and headed back to the lodge and he thought she was probably on to him then. It took him a long time to lie his way back. That, he told himself, was the final time. And sure, he'd told himself "final time" before, only to have the thing behind his gut, the dragon that lived in the basement start demanding food—but this time he meant it. He was going to let the damn thing starve.

But a starving dragon is loud. It knocks things from the walls and this was a bad season for it, a bad year. It would be a tough time for Maranda while he let it all bleed from his system, and this seemed like a bad few months for her, she wasn't ready, and so eventually he decided to just go ahead and go back to it. To keep his equilibrium. That was the trip last week, the one she caught him on.

Jesus. How did he ever think this was something she would not only understand, but appreciate?

They drive and drive. He keeps checking the pistol in the back. The sun is nothing more than a vague shape in the sky.

He's not sure if he should be calling Maranda his wife or not. He wants to, but does she think of him as her husband? What exactly is he to her? Are they still legitimately married if the only reason is that there aren't operable divorce courts?

They're going to get Gracie. That's the focus, and the only hope of a way back to her. Maybe it'll show her he's changed. Like, in rescuing Gracie, he might rescue his own marriage too. Or is he still using her? No longer as a sex object, but as the proof of his own absolution? No, he's heroic, right? A modern knight. His quest is to protect her through fire and danger until they've reached Gracie and *then...*

Then what? He'll be seen and known, forgiven and accepted, and she'll be healed by his knightly devotion? Christ, he's maybe never been more ridiculous.

Keep driving, he tells himself. Keep moving forward, that's all there is to do.

The road here is oceanically buckled. The air above looks like it's still loading.

Up ahead is what appears to be a massive boulder, black and sharp-edged and taking up most of the road. Ben actually thinks for a moment that it's an enormous meteorite, that this is *it*, the cause of the cataclysm, and it has somehow landed and done this much damage to the surrounding forest without making even an impact crater.

But as they get closer, he sees it's a tractor-trailer jackknifed across both lanes. There are soot-streaks down the sides. The tires are melted. There's still someone in the cab. As Ben slows to drive past, he tries not to look, but how can you not? It's a black skeleton, no clothes or hair at all. Face drawn in a meatless grin. Ben stops, rolls his window down, like the guy might have something to say.

Later, Maranda drives. There are bottles and wrappers all over the console and front seats. Ben leans back in the passenger seat with his shoes off, stealing glances at her.

He couldn't figure her out before, so how could he now? How can you get your arms around that much past and wrestle it into any sort of cohesive shape to even *understand*, much less help dismantle? She's a wall that goes on forever. No footholds, no breaks in the brick.

He's got no plan, no idea what he's doing. All he can think is that he wants to hear her talk.

"What's she like?" he asks.

"Gracie?"

"Yeah," Ben says. "Like, what do you remember?"

MARANDA

What does she remember? She remembers too much—that's the issue, isn't it? Her head's a solar system chock full of rogue bodies and planet-bombs. Flaming gas and dead aliens. It'll shred your skin to ribbons.

But at the same time there are those in-between places where it's all nothingness and void. Like, for example, why doesn't she remember anything—with one absolutely fucked-up exception—before age eight?

That's a hole you could get lost in real quick, kid.

Axel's right. Maranda shakes her head, tries to refocus.

Gracie though, Gracie she remembers well.

"I think they were grooming her," she says. "They get kids, runaways, foster-care, whatever. Get them ready. She's probably as old now as I was when…"

She comes right to the wall, hardly realizing it. The point of no return. She takes a second and backs herself up, but it has gravity. You get too close and before you know it it's pulling on you and the floor has turned to ice.

Ben doesn't say anything as she takes a breath and mentally backpedals. She's glad for not having to explain.

"I couldn't get her out with me. I wanted to go back but I…I couldn't."

The road's yellow lines skate by beneath them. Ben scratches his nose.

"For a while, at the beginning, she wouldn't stop crying. Just on and on and on. Shit, it was horrible. But I gave her *this*"—she holds up the rabbit—"and for whatever reason, it helped."

She watches Ben out of the corner of her eye as he leans back, nodding. Lately, there's something different about him. Guys are predatory—in some part of their brain they want to lick your blood off their fingers—but Ben at least seems genuinely to be resisting it. If there was a way, she gets the sense he'd maybe have that part cut out.

"What else?" he asks.

She remembers being in a basement, a few of the girls lying around, one of them smoking. That dreamy haze of dust. Maranda sitting on the floor with Gracie.

"I'd play on the floor with her," she tells him. "I'd balance a spoon on my nose. When she'd grab at it, I'd snatch it away and say, 'No!' She laughed like a maniac."

Ben smiles to himself, holding one foot in his lap.

"Or, okay, one time I came home from, like, whatever, and I'd been able to sneak some contraband."

"Contraband?"

"Yeah," she laughs. "Dinner rolls. A kid's menu. One of those, you know, the cheap crayons."

He laughs. "The primary colors?"

"Right, exactly. The ones that break if you press too hard."

"You stole those?"

"Hell yeah I did! I'm a good…color-er? Is that a word? Whatever, I'm good at coloring. Gracie lit up when I showed her so it was like, okay, we're coloring then."

God, it's actually *fun* for a second, talking about this. It's the best she's felt in a while. She can feel Chipmunk pressing from the inside, a little *tap tap tap*.

Maranda takes a breath and shrugs. Sure, Chipmunk. Why not? She yields the floor, easy as anything.

From the inside, it's like she's watching out her own eyes as Chipmunk emerges, her voice chirpy and small.

"Me and Gracie are the same number of years old, both six, and Gracie's *my* best friend, not Maranda's. So I wanna tell some."

She can see Ben's face soften. He smiles and says, "Okay, go ahead."

She wonders if he's able to look through Chipmunk and see her, Maranda. Though, does it even matter? She talks and talks, telling him anything that comes to mind, her mouth forming words some other brain is making.

"One time we were lying on our stomachs on the floor, and the floors there smelled sometimes, I'm not sure what they smelled like, but sometimes they smelled, like the outside when it is hot and you're in a city, mean—but when you have crayons and a book then it smells like that instead. And we colored a picture of a man who was a milkshake and he had a hat and arms and legs and his body was a cup. It was one of the best ones, one of the very very good ones. But Gracie laughed because even though I do my best people sometimes laugh at me. But then Gracie said it wasn't me she was laughing at, because she's my best friend and she was laughing in a fun way. She said, 'You're funny mommy,' and then she had her hand over her mouth and she was laughing and I was laughing too, and then we both laughed even harder."

All at once Maranda's back. It's smooth, like she's only stepped into another room, still within easy reach if she wants to say something.

The memory's not one she could recall herself, but as Chipmunk tells the story she can see it, remembering and experiencing at once.

She realizes she's still driving. Forgot about *that* when she gave Chipmunk the reigns. Not her smartest move. But apparently…it was okay?

Guardian says, *Taken care of. I got you, kid.*

Maranda experiences a surge. A blend of competence and gratitude. Like she could do anything.

They've not seen a single person for going on 48 hours, not since the Farnsworth's RV, when two military Humvees roar up behind from out of nowhere. She can feel the rumble in her pelvis, the engines throaty as subterranean thunder. They file past in the other lane and accelerate into the distance.

"Must be getting close," Ben says.

"I guess so."

For maybe a full minute, silence falls over them. It's awkward, but then it grows comfortable and warm and the pressure to come up with something to say more or less evaporates.

Well, we're doing all right, aren't we? Klara says.

Maranda gives a sniff-laugh. The corner of her mouth turns up.

"What?" Ben asks.

The tundra is mottled with sunlight. Here and there she sees bursts of green. "I don't know," she says. "Just…despite everything, *someone* in there is feeling good about things. I think I am too."

A few moments pass, and then Maranda lets Klara out. Just for a minute. Even here at the wrong end of the telescope, she feels what Klara does. The weight of the car, how good it is to move and control it. And strongly, the desire for Ben to say her name.

Smoke is lingering beyond the mountains, wide and loose like a rope coming undone at the top. Here and there are openings, gashes of light.

Ben knows who they are now. This is a new thing. If people know you, your name, they can call you out and it is not good to hand over power to someone. And yet, Klara wants it, and Maranda's surprised to find she does too. She wants him to know her. She wants a way for them to make things right. She wants him to look at her and see her. To know her, and say her name.

BEN

Mile after mile of black. Each tree is whittled down to its barest, shriveled core. Him too, it feels like. He's emptied out. Nothing but himself.

When they stop to switch drivers, he notices her watching him and then lowering her eyes when he looks back. It's like she wants to make sure he's still there.

He realizes who it is at the same instant he says it: "Klara."

She looks down, biting her lip. She opens and closes her hands in her lap.

"I am…sorry," she says.

"I know."

"Is just…I want *risk.* I want *danger.*"

He realizes, before he even says anything, that in his heart he's already laid the whole matter with David to rest. It's settled and done. He motions with his head out the window, at the darkness and smoke.

"This isn't dangerous enough?"

It takes Klara a moment to realize he's joking. "Yes. Yes, you're right." She touches the corners of her eyes, then reaches into her purse for a menthol, but doesn't light it. "Just, *fun* risk. That kind."

"Yeah, I know. I get it," he says, and does.

As she takes the cigarette between her lips, bending her head to light it, he gives the accelerator a little goose, for the hell of it. She sits up, looking around, and lowers the lighter. He does it again, this time steadying the pedal toward the floor.

Klara frowns, looking at him, but he pretends to be studying the road. He's only able to hold it a moment though, before he breaks. Klara punches his arm.

He lifts his palms to see the speedometer needle rising. Seventy-five. Ninety. Higher. He's never driven this fast before, and shit—it's fun. Klara is gripping the handle above the door and holds his elbow with the other, and that feels good. A squeal escapes her. As they crest a hill, Route 1 becomes a straightaway and it feels for a moment like they might get airborne. Everything lifts weightlessly in his stomach, and he can see for miles and miles ahead.

As they come down the edge of Nalchina they keep seeing papers scattered alongside the road. They round a bend and come upon a whole flock of them.

Ben pulls onto the shoulder. It's like a wind tunnel. The documents are pasted madly about the road, like God thought to wallpaper the whole mountain but abandoned the project. Every time the wind blows they lift and live and die all over again.

Ben chases one down and catches it underfoot. There's scorch on the edges. Birthdays, dates of service, social security numbers. He snags another spiked to a tree and it's more of the same.

"I think they're health insurance documents," he calls. "Musta been a truck."

Maranda shrugs. "Doesn't really matter now I guess." She motions with her head toward the promontory, and he follows her out.

Below them, the valley shines with melt. There's a shelf of ice way back in the mountain pass.

"It's Matanuska," he whispers.

Maranda nods. "The lookout."

He's seen pictures of it, but he can't reconcile those images with what he's seeing now. The glacier's all but gone, everything out there is flooded and dark.

"It can't be," he says, even though it is, and he knows it.

There are three quarter-operated viewfinders mounted on the railing, all heat-twisted and dark. Maranda tries, but none of them will take a coin.

They stand side by side holding the railing. The distant mountains are granitic and black. The forest in the distance nothing but burn and little ribbons of smoke. It looks like an invisible army has dotted the land with cook fires.

"We'll be in Anchorage tomorrow," she says.

It feels strange to talk about it. They hardly have, as if the prospects of this are so delicate that by saying it aloud they might chase it off.

Ben turns. Her face is focused and grim in the light. "We could make it tonight," he says. "If we wanted. If this is Matanuska, we're only a hundred miles out."

"Let's wait for morning. Attack it in daylight."

Hesitantly, he puts his arm behind her back. They stand there together, on the verge of something, he feels, but he doesn't know of what. Only that things are about to break—one way or another.

That evening, Ben takes out a blanket and lays it with a flourish across the roof of the Audi, inviting her to sit with a little waiter-ly gesture.

"Thank you," she laughs.

He sets out four bottles of water, assorted leftover cans.

"Real spoons," he says.

"An apocalyptic picnic, huh?"

"You got it. Green beans, or ravioli?"

She decides on both, and they eat more than they've let themselves the entire trip. He doesn't even notice the metallic taste anymore. Maranda tilts up her last can to spoon out the bottom, then leans back on her hands to watch the evening fall.

"Maybe things are better south," she says.

"They can't get worse."

"Knock on wood." She makes a show of looking around for wood until Ben taps the side of his head. It's dumb, but she laughs.

"It's probably beautiful down there," he says. "What with the messed-up weather. Tropical Oregon."

"I could do Oregon."

A little fist tightens in Ben's chest when she says *I*. He wipes his mouth on the back of his arm, offering her a water bottle. She takes a swig and hands it back.

"I mean, like, when you say *I* you mean…"

Maranda shrugs. "I don't know," she says. "I just, who knows?"

When they got married, just over a year ago, she'd made the exact same expression looking out at the mostly empty courthouse room, his tie just right and she in a one-armed dress. He hadn't realized, back then, how goddamn happy he'd actually been.

He looks at her, and for once she doesn't look away. Even through all the time of him trying to escape her, seeking out others, even when he told himself she had no effect on him, she still did. Still does.

Down below, the Matanuska is colossal and slow. The mountains are knifed with orange.

He doesn't want to fix or save her, only to stay near. She's a fire; by night, enough to walk by. After all this time, all he wants is to see his life—whatever remains of it— unfold alongside her. He's being selfish, of course, but maybe she wants that too. Maybe.

Powerfully, he feels the urge to kiss her. It feels like it's coming from a non-fragmented place, a small intact part that is pulsing and whole. They haven't kissed since, Jesus, he doesn't even know since when.

"What?" she smiles.

He lowers his head, looks away. "Nothing," he laughs. The moment passes, which is maybe for the better. They're still so delicate. But it feels like if he did lean in that close to her again, he'd fall in all the way. Just fall and fall and fall.

MARANDA

They stop at an already-looted rest area outside Palmer. Getting out of the car, Maranda can hear everybody now. She's full of their voices, like a steady, nurturing rain.

The storm of her people, is it over? She's terrified, but also not afraid at all. If so, maybe now they can get down—together—to the business at hand.

Inside the rest stop, there are wet travel brochures pulped all over the lobby floor. In one corner is a grimy coffee maker. In another a tipped-over vending machine with footprints across the back.

Ben gets down with his face against the floor and comes up with a few candy bars and a bag of pretzels. As he claps the dirt from his chest and stomach, Maranda walks up behind him, trailing her fingers down his back. She's got lightning in her hands, that's how good she feels. When he looks at her, she plucks the pretzels from him and heads for the restroom. She can feel him staring as she opens the bag.

"Be right back," she sings, popping one in her mouth.

So much of what they started out with was complete shit, but she knows the worst of him now. And he of her. There's something to be said for that—for choosing one person and allowing the entirety of them to seep into you. Who knows? Maybe the winds are changing.

In the bathroom, the walls are scalloped with mud. One of the mirrors is split diagonally, the lower half shattered all over the floor. She palms two pumps of soap and lathers her hands, but when she tries the faucet the pipes shudder in the walls, and no water comes out.

Ben sticks his head in, winks. "Coffee works. Want a cup?"

She wipes her hands as clean as she can on the back of her pants. "You're trespassing," she says. "But sure."

She holds out the belly of her shirt. The fabric is stretched, pinholed with burns. There's a brown scythe-shape that might be blood but she doesn't know from when, or who.

She can hear Klara plain as day: *Oh, it's a lousy outfit anyway, dear.*

She can't help but chuckle. Klara's not as bad as she used to think.

Leaning in, she turns her face one way, then another. She looks different from each side, or if she tilts her head up or down. Like each twist reveals another face.

What's up? Axel says, and she swears she can see him. It feels like if she did this long enough she could see them all. Past and present, all together.

Ordinarily, the story of her escape seems hardly worth telling. It's just a transition, as anti-climactic as crossing an unmarked border. But today she's found herself thinking about it.

Back then, home was a scummy apartment in Anchorage. Five of the wifeys and Luke, Louise visiting from time to time, like she was Mother Theresa or something.

Maranda had been in the bathroom upstairs, looking at a still-raised mark behind her ear where Luke had hit her the night before. She'd thought he was going to kill her. He'd said the words before—usually that meant he was going to fuck you, or beat you, maybe both, but last night he wasn't even mad. Just said, "Okay, choose," and laid out a screwdriver, a saw, and a gun. She was high as hell (*did he know? Did the fucker get her high to keep the Axel-voices from getting out?*) but she still knew enough to pick the gun.

The worst part wasn't her teeth scraping metal when he made her pretend to blow it, the worst part was finally getting *through* the vomiting and the millions of hornets that were going to burst out of her, getting to the place in her head where it was quiet and calm and she could accept what was about to happen—she was going to die, he was going to pull the trigger and everything was going to *pop* and that would be it, the end, and it would be here, in Anchorage, and nobody would know, or care—the worst part was getting through all of that and then having him change his mind, smack her, fuck her, and go to bed.

The next morning nothing felt real. She was a bomb that hadn't landed yet.

In the upstairs bathroom, lifting a frond of oily, wet-blonde hair, she'd realized even the gash on her scalp wasn't hers. Everything about her was somebody else's.

That was when a voice in her head said: *Out the window.* They didn't lock anything, Luke and Louise had them all so mind-bent they more or less guarded themselves. No bars like invisible ones. Only now, looking back, can she tell this tiny, out-of-nowhere push must have been Guardian. It was time to either run or die.

She hesitated, and Axel barked, *Now. You have to do it now.*

There were other voices too, telling her to wait, telling her to think about Gracie or telling her that *this* was her life, *the* life, she wasn't gonna find another man who cared even as much as Luke did, but all she heard clearly were the first ones, Axel and Guardian pushing her on and so she did it. She opened the bathroom window.

Outside, the air was blue and cold. She was straddling the window in a silk bathrobe, listening to the wind scraping the streets. Openness stretched in every direction. In all likelihood, she was going to get caught, but Luke was going to kill her anyway, so what the hell?

She looked back at the door. Imagined Luke bursting in, a bullet carving the butter of her skull. Or maybe he'd pull her in by the ankle, crack her head against the toilet. Or just—*bop*—quick shove, out the window sideways and it would be a long feeling, falling like that, until the road finally came up and punched out her breath.

Guardian and a few of the others said: *Now. Do it.*

She swung a leg out, holding the edge with her fingertips. The street was empty and no one noticed her drop, bare feet slapping in the dark. She closed herself off and ran. Ran and ran and ran and ran.

Back in the present, in the rest stop's bathroom, she combs a hand through her hair, now dark and short.

Enough, she thinks. She's ready. Her chest is wild. It's pulsing and free.

No more running.

BEN

As Route 1 opens to four lanes, Ben sits up in the passenger seat and rubs his face. There are people camping in the fields, vehicles converging from the outlying towns. But through it all, he feels different. Cleaned out and new.

Most of the cars look blown out of hell—rims scraping, scorch all down the sides. One's going on three tires. Others have cartop carriers bungeed almost-shut, or mattresses strapped to their roofs. Most of them, he and Maranda included, are treating the speed limit like it's little more than a quaint triviality, which is maybe exactly what it is.

There's a Ford making a heavy ripping sound down the middle of the highway. Maranda merges as far as she can to the left but it still almost swipes them.

"Jesus," Ben mumbles, watching it veer back and forth across the lanes.

On the radio, someone's still giving periodic reports: *"NASA is monitoring NEOs…experts…the Yellowstone Caldera, which could be threatening…"*

A purl of white noise washes up. He waits but it doesn't clear. It's all the same anyway. Nothing's changed for days now. He reaches up and clicks it off. Nobody has any idea what's going on.

They pass under a sign: ANCHORAGE—30 MILES. Maranda looks at him and takes his hand. She narrows her eyes and takes a long breath, like she's about to dive underwater.

Coming down through the Chugach mountains, they pull onto the shoulder and switch sides. Maranda hesitates before getting back in.

"Look," she motions. Way in the distance, through the haze, Ben can make out a few squat shapes against the mountains.

It's Anchorage, he realizes. Behind it, the Knik Arm is the same cantaloupe color of the sky.

"Look at that," he says.

"I wasn't sure we'd get here."

For a moment, he imagines himself breaking down a door, or shooting someone. Could he shoot someone? Yeah. Hell yeah he could. They'd start pleading and he'd just say, "Shut up," and pull the trigger.

A tractor trailer passes close enough that its horn blast rattles the Audi's windows. About stops his heart.

Ben sniffs, shakes himself back to reality. Maranda's watching him.

"You ready?" she asks.

PART III

MARANDA

As they drive the last miles into the city, she starts getting colder and colder. She can feel the newer voice, the mean one, gathering within.

Don't forget, the voice says. *You're nothing. Remember all those years here, the life? Being nothing is how you survived. It's dangerous to be something. Look around. People, buildings. All something. All ready to break.*

Everything—she, Ben, the whole planet—it's all sanding itself down to raw. It feels like her bones might freeze and shatter.

Who are you? Maranda thinks.

There's a black sun about to rise, the cold voice says. *It's gonna come up and start swallowing.*

Shut up.

But the voice just laughs. *The trick is biding your time,* it says. *The trick is knowing when it's right.*

BEN

Anchorage is swarming. The streets are choked, cars either abandoned or stuck in gridlock. Some are inching forward onto the sidewalks and scraping against concrete. Electrical cables are strung above the streets like laundry line, holding spray-painted banners and appeals for help and here and there proclamations of the end.

Ben locks the doors. Even inside the car you can smell it—too many people in one place. They're on rooftops, beside the roads, running through traffic crosswise. A boy of maybe ten is running up and over cars in his bare feet. Every available surface has a tent on it. Someone's got firewood on the sidewalk, jostling a cooking pan over a tiny flame. They drive past a storefront covered with plywood and spray-painted FUCK U.

On one corner he sees a white-haired man in a baseball hat, tufts mushrooming over his ears. He's wearing army fatigues and a white signboard: ARE YOU READY YET?? As they pass, the guy makes eye contact with Ben and touches his hat.

There's a sporadic military presence. A soldier on a corner holding an M4. Police barricades, officers unloading riot shields from the back of a van. Ben touches Maranda's shoulder and nods to indicate a tank.

"Not how I remember it," Maranda says.

"I bet not."

"It looks like a refugee camp. How many people you think are here?"

Ben whistles. "Who knows. Say a million. What's Anchorage's population?"

"I don't know. A quarter that?"

Ben leans forward. It's only noon, maybe, but already the sky is a deep twilight color. The gathering clouds are purple and sharp.

In a truck stop parking lot, Luke takes his jacket and shirt off and palms most of a water bottle over his chest and shoulders, then pours the rest over his head, glancing at himself in the window. He's well-muscled, mapped with tattoos. There's a rosary inked around his neck and an open-mouthed dragon wrapped around his ribcage.

The place is overrun with shelter-seekers. A few people walking to their cars eye him uneasily. When he's dry he puts his shirt back on and climbs into the driver's seat.

"She good back there?"

His partner finishes climbing over the console, scratching as always. He straightens his shirt and lowers the visor. The look of a man recently fed. "Now she is."

They take Whitney to Ocean Dock past warehouses, a depot, chemical silos. They drive over downed powerlines. The nearby trains are sitting on the ties.

The Port itself is an everliving clusterfuck. The water's choked with cruise liners and bulk carriers. Cranes abandoned mid-load. There are crowds all over the docks.

Each of the ramps has at least one cop stationed at the bottom with a riot shield, but the one in front of the orange carrier is safe people. Luke gets out and slings the unconscious girl over his shoulder. When he walks past the cop he motions with his head at the girl like, what are you going to do? and keeps going.

The side of the ship is stenciled with its name: MAYA III.

MARANDA

Her heart is like a hummingbird. God it's going. She tries to will it down before it strangles her. She remembers everything here. Every stick, every stone.

What, Axel says, *did you think it wouldn't be like this?*

She says, out loud, "Shut up."

Ben glances at her, stung.

"Sorry," she mumbles.

Seriously though, shut up.

Axel grunts, *Ah whatever.*

Enough, Guardian says. *Take a left here.*

She worked there and there and there. All these places. That track, that blade. From I to G on 6th Ave, the back end of 7th.

The cold voice is singing, over and over, *Slut slut slut slut slut slut slut.*

Maranda feels ridiculous trying to avert her eyes from stoplights and bakeries, but she's afraid of the iron core way back in her stomach. If she makes eye contact with anything it's going to magnetize, pull her right in.

They pass a group on a street corner with handkerchiefs knotted around their heads and their hands in the air. Somebody holds up a bundle of tinfoil with a rope and lights it. Green smoke goes everywhere.

Ben keeps touching the handgun in his lap. "You know where?" he asks.

She nods. Of course she knows where. It's coded into her goddamn bones.

A dead-end street. A few brick apartments and a beige condo. The road's littered with trash and the powerlines are sagging almost to the ground, but otherwise it looks normal enough.

Blood's thrumming in her ears. She has to try twice to get any words out.

"Here," she says. "That condo."

Ben wipes his mouth. "That?"

"Yeah." She squeezes the wheel. "You sure about this?"

Ben nods. "They *can't* see you. I go in, pretend. See what I find."

She's going to vomit. Her guts are going to get pulled right out, flung all over the car. She's going to float into space, sucked up and away into some incredible black hole.

"Listen," she says. "When you walk in, you have to…" but then stops, realizing. "Never mind," she says.

Honestly, right now she's just happy she doesn't have to talk.

"I got this," Ben says. He kisses her cheek and gets out. He points at the gun, which he's left in the front seat, until she makes eye contact.

"Okay," she says, but he's already out the door, jogging toward the condo. She swallows. Her throat's shredded trying to hold it all in, trying to keep herself nailed to the earth.

BEN

The condo's automatic doors shudder open. He's trying to hurry and still look casual, before the inner resources he's gathered can be un-gathered.

Inside, the place looks empty. The one light still on at the end of the lobby flicks chaotically and then goes off. There are papers strewn across the floor and a flipped-over polyester couch. About a third of the brushed nickel mailbox doors are open, some with keys still in the lock.

Is this the wrong place? Or maybe everyone's already gone? All at once he feels the craziness of it, the needle-in-the-haystack absurdity of finding one girl in all of Anchorage.

When the light at the other end of the lobby buzzes back on, he can see the shadow of another hallway to the left. He jogs forward, to see, just so he can be positively certain before he has to go out here in a second and tell Maranda no dice.

Turning the corner, Ben about runs into a guy. He's wearing black sweats and stops Ben by putting a hand on his chest.

All right then, Ben thinks. Here we go.

"Can I help you?" the guy says, chewing gun. His accent's meaty. He's got on runners the same brand as his outfit.

Ben sniffs, wipes his nose. He tries to adopt a certain demeanor, but it's forced, and he's pretty sure it shows. He pulls both sides of the collar to straighten his jacket.

"Yeah, I got a buddy in town. I wanna show him a good time before...you know." He motions outside. "Whatever the hell happens."

The man leans, scans the lobby. He looks back at Ben and raises an eyebrow.

"Yeah, well, he'll be here later. I wanna see if this is a place worth bringing him, you know?"

The man doesn't move except for his jaw.

Ben holds his jacket open, turns a slow circle. "What, you wanna frisk me?"

There's a moment where Ben can't tell if he's going to get decked or not, but then the man moves the gum over to the side of his mouth and turns around.

"Come," he says.

The room Ben gets let into is filled floor to ceiling with music. It takes hold of your lungs and starts hand-pumping. Everything's lit blue. The first thing Ben sees is a girl in her underwear sprawled on a couch against the opposite wall. He feels everything tighten, from his throat all the way down to his groin, and a precipice opens up at his toes. It leads all the way down, he knows. He also knows that before he hit bottom there'd be a whole lot he'd enjoy the absolute hell out of.

No, he thinks, clamping down. *No.*

The girl's touching the couch's fabric with the backs of her fingers, following with her eyes some invisible trail across the ceiling. High as hell, Ben realizes.

At the kitchen bar two other girls are leaning forward, drinking by turns from the same travel mug. They look at him with absolutely no expression. In the other corner is a fourth girl with a baby-faced guy who can't be any more than, what, like nineteen? He's sucking a vape and he tips his head back to laugh belatedly at his own joke, vapor coming out in a jagged, broken stream.

Ben wipes his hands on his legs. Tries to look like he just happens to be standing here and, oh sure, now that you mention it, yeah, he does need a hook-up, thanks.

"Welcome welcome, cowboy," the kid says, disentangling from the girl and sauntering over. "Take a load off."

"Nice place."

The kid erupts like this is some great joke. He looks around and it only gets funnier. "Right? *Right?* What can I do you for, brother?"

It's the way he says "brother." Like everyone's a part of this. It makes Ben want to rip his throat out, but instead he forces a laugh and looks around. One of the girls at the bar has her head down, but the other watches him.

Ben coughs. He tries to play it just the right degree of casual. "Any…younger?"

The kid raises his eyebrows. Blows vapor out sideways. "How young?"

"Depends what you've got."

He knows the game. Hands over a few bills. The kid puts them away and clicks his tongue.

"Wait here."

Ben's shaking. The room's getting smaller. He can feel the dragon behind his navel. Maybe this was a mistake. He's not brave, and he's nowhere near as changed as he wants to be.

MARANDA

She cycles through the radio station by station, hardly aware of what she's doing, just trying to get her mind to a place where she can breathe. There's nothing to find anyway. She goes from one end of the band to the other, static rising and falling like waves—in and out and in and out.

Everything's watching her. Every window, every car. Even the trees have eyes. This place has too much to say.

It says: *I KNOW YOU.*

It says: *SLUT.*

It says: *READY TO COME BACK?*

Her every sense is bent around anticipating the sound of Ben opening the door. When something blots out the light, she assumes it's him and puts her hand on the shifter, but then a shadow falls across her. She's been parked in by a black SUV. She tries to get out, tries to run, but the guy already has the door open, and then something heavy lands on the back of her head.

Her brain gets hole-punched. *Ker-chunk.* A few moments are just gone.

She's being dragged by the elbows. Something hits her again and she doesn't feel it, not at all. She only hears the sound, and for a second she can't move her arms.

Shit, Axel growls. Someone else in there is screaming until he barks, *Shut up!*

Her lower half lands heavy on the pavement. He doesn't even lift her, just drags her by the wrists across the asphalt.

A door slams. Another.

As she falls further and further away, she can feel Axel taking over.

Okay, he says, *that's okay. Wrists are already zip-tied. Ankles too...*

Fuck.

Not again. No, not again.

Again? Maranda has time to think, but it's like she's half-asleep. Axel pushes her out of the way, like he's taking the wheel mid-road. Then the car starts moving and she smells cologne, antiseptic.

Yeah, Axel says. *This is Luke's car.*

BEN

As soon as the pimp walks out the door, Ben rushes over to the two girls at the bar.

"I need your help," he says. "I'm looking for a girl."

The one raises her eyebrows, takes a drink.

"No, little. Young. Six, seven, I don't know. Gracie. You know her?"

The girl looks at him.

"She's…not…for, no. Not for that. It's…my wife…"

She glances at the other girl, who exhales and moves away.

"Where? Where would they keep her?"

Just then the door in the back opens and Ben steps back, straightening his shirt. The kid comes in all smiles.

"There's a…there's a wait for the fresh ones," he says, hands held out apologetically. "We've got a private, you know, like another place. And it's, uh, a little more."

Ben scratches the underside of his chin. He's not getting anywhere this way. He glances at the exits. There's probably a guy or two out in the hall, but there hasn't been anybody else in or out since he arrived. Just this guy and four girls.

"Well," Ben says.

He's only dimly aware of what he's about to do, but there's no time for waiting anymore. All right, Ben thinks.

This is happening now. Vaguely surprised at himself, he grabs hold of the kid's jersey and yanks him toward the door.

"Hey, listen…" the kid says.

"Shut up."

The half-stoned girl on the couch twists her head and laughs. The one at the bar is the only one who makes eye contact with Ben, but she doesn't say or do anything more. He elbows the door open behind him and heads right.

The lights in the hallway are winking erratically. He's got the kid bent over almost double, one arm chicken winged up close to his neck.

"Fuck you man!" the kid yells.

Up ahead is an exit sign pointing around a corner. Ben pushes the kid ahead of him and shoulder-charges around the bend, but there's no need—the hallway's completely deserted. Just a few doors hanging open, and at the end a blinking EXIT sign.

Outside, everything is bright and open and hot. It half-blinds him. They're in a side lot with three or four dumpsters. A siren far off. He pulls the kid against the building, heart hammering, and they make their way around to the Audi.

It's running, but no one's in it. Maranda isn't there.

Everything he's been holding together is flying apart.

Ben yanks the kid to his feet. A reptile crawls into his head.

"Where is she?" he barks.

The kid spits on him. "Fuck you."

Ben closes his eyes. The spittle slides down his nose, but he refuses to wipe it off. His body swells, deflates, swells, deflates. He's done getting screwed over. He opens his eyes and at the same time sweeps the kid's feet out from under him. The kid drops like his legs are gone, and something hits pavement with a hollow knock. Ben kicks him once in the gut. A ferocity that surprises even him.

He hears himself yelling, "You really wanna do this, motherfucker? Do you?"

The kid's head snaps back. He groans and a little blood-bubble comes out. Ben wheels back but before he can kick something encircles him and he's in the air, kicking nothing, and then he's back on the ground and a tremendous force hits him in the stomach. It feels like he's been impaled, that's the first thing he thinks—speared through by a telephone pole. Everything in his vision goes red and bends. He tries to get up but there aren't any solid surfaces. The pimp's lying next to him looking at the sky. Then Ben's on his back and the guy from the lobby is over him, and what scares him the most is the look on the guy's face. He's not sweating or straining, no emotion at all, like this is just something he's doing and then he'll go and do something else. A hellsky drifts behind him. Ben can't do anything but wait for it, but then a little cloud erupts on the back of the guy's head and he blinks, frowning. His one eye drifts sideways, then corrects itself, and a brick punches him a second time on the cheek and he goes down.

Something falls onto Ben's shirt. He blinks at it, trying to focus. A tooth. There's a pink shred of gum still attached.

He can feel his heartbeat in his face. He leans up on an elbow and sees a woman kneeling nearby. It takes him a moment, things are foggy, but it's the girl from inside, from the kitchen. It looks like she's pounding something with a rock, like Stone Age cornmeal grinding or whatever, but then he sees the kid's feet and realizes she's atomizing his face.

"Fucking…fuck, *suka, blyat*…FUCKFACE!"

There's blood all up and down her arm. She gives a final yell and stands, spikes the brick. She turns toward the Audi.

"Come on," she says to Ben. "Get in."

Every length of street is choked with traffic. Horns are going everywhere. People cross in droves. The lights, amazingly, still work, though they might as well be off. Cars make their way in lurches while others idle. A shimmer of exhaust hangs in the air.

Ben's in the back, pressing a t-shirt to his nose. The girl—woman? he doesn't know what to call her—seems unperturbed. She mounts a curb to get around two wrecked cars, then bangs down on the other side. It sends a flash through his skull, and he white-knuckles the door handle as she makes a hard turn against the light on 3rd, into the biking lane.

Out the window, a group of maybe eight people have been hanged in a line from the arm of a construction crane.

"Alyona," the woman says. Her accent's strong. "My name."

It takes Ben a moment to pull his gaze from the bodies. "Oh, uh—Ben." He takes the shirt away from his face, looks down his nose at the blood-bloom, then puts it back.

"They are at harbor," Alyona says.

"Both of them?"

She doesn't answer. Ben presses an imaginary brake as she squeals to a stop just a few feet from the waiting traffic ahead of them. His head throbs.

"Why the…why the harbor? No one's allowed to leave."

"Second place there. That's where people are. Business doesn't stop." She says it *busy-ness*, shaking her head.

Outside, tents are set up all over and where there aren't tents people are in sleeping bags or tucked into alleyways. There's a guy walking a Pomeranian, which is fucking nuts. On the corner, three men are screaming at a soldier who isn't reacting to them at all.

"It is bulk carrier," Alyona continues, pulling around a van, which draws a blast on its horn. "Maya III. Some being sold off. Others…"

Ben's not sure what that's supposed to mean. He tongues the inside of his lip.

"Why are you helping me?"

Alyona twists the corner of her mouth. "I…I want to help. Maybe, maybe first good thing I get to do. Who knows, maybe last too."

"I know the feeling."

"People saying it is end of world. You think?"

Ben leans over, glances into the sky. "It's *something*."

There's a fire in a trash barrel. A circle of women chanting. Beyond it, Ben sees the Pilot.

He sits up. "That's her."

The street is two lanes each way, curbed down the middle. The black Pilot's right there, not ninety feet ahead. Maybe a half dozen cars between them.

"Hold on," Alyona says, but before Ben even has time to she's got the Audi up on the meridian. Ben palms the roof, presses both his feet into the floor. A few horns blare from opposing traffic, the squeal of rubber and brakes. Alyona guns it, runneling swaths of mud out of the landscaping. At the next light she jerks the wheel and they're back in the flow of traffic, just behind and adjacent to the Pilot.

"All right," Ben says. "Now…"

"I ram it," Alyona interrupts. It's not a question.

Ben watches her through the mirror, realizes he's not afraid at all. Everything's happening at a comfortable distance and speed.

He nods. "Do it."

MARANDA

Axel's the one in control right now, but little tendrils of the outside world—her face against the carpet in the back of the car—bleed into her mind. Underneath the cologne, there's a tang you can smell. Sweet and gamey. It hits her like a backhand, what it is.

They raped somebody back here.

She feels drugged. Not a body at all. A tunnel crowds her vision.

Easy now, Axel says. *It ain't gonna happen. Not again.*

She's still able to watch as Axel readjusts in the backseat, trying to get his zip-tied arms back far enough that he can get his feet through them.

"Yo," the guy says, just a little lackey of a kid. "Hey, cut that. You hear me? You want fucked up?"

"Yeah," Axel growls, his voice out of her throat. "I want you to hit me, bitch."

The guy's voice shoots up like a bottle rocket. "What the *hell?*"

Then the world shatters. Collapses sideways, and she's airborne. She feels Axel trying to get her hands up, but they're still tied.

BEN

Alyona only hesitates a fraction of a second. Ben has just enough time to grab hold of the seat-back before she closes her eyes and jerks the wheel.

There's a heavy *thunck* as the front of the Audi connects with the driver's side of the Pilot. You can feel the front of the car give way. They start spinning.

Ben sees in flashes. Other cars swerving. There's an even harder jolt as they hit a light pole, and his head comes off the window. He doesn't actually remember hitting it, but he can feel pressure under the skin that will soon become pain. The seatbelt feels like a baseball bat that just got him in the chest.

Alyona's sits up and pushes hair out of her face. Every window is white smoke. Somewhere nearby is the sound of other cars colliding.

"You alright?" Ben says.

"I think so."

Through the smoke, he can see the guy get out of the Pilot. Ben's whole body tightens. The guy spits blood into his hand and wipes it on the ass of his jeans. He draws a gun—Ben's gun—and stumbles toward them, rub-scratching his neck.

"The fuck man?" he yells. "What the actual fuck?"

"Get down," Ben whispers to Alyona. "Don't move."

He locks the passenger door, then crouches lower in the backseat, just as the guy smacks the window and starts jiggling the door. Ben can see the hair on his face, his bleeding lower lip. Ben eases the latch on the door handle and holds it, ready.

When the guy moves to the back door, Ben jerks it open. Gets him right in the face. The guy stumbles, clutching his nose, and Ben kicks so the door hits him again. There's blood streaming down each wrist. Ben's out and on him immediately. A quick punch to the head and then he goes for the gun. That's all he's thinking: get the gun. He shoulders him, gets him back against the Audi, but even with his face bloodied to hell, the guy won't let go. He tries forcing it toward the guy's foot, but then there's an enormous flat bang. Ben stumbles back a step. He thinks he can feel something ricochet against his shin, but as soon as he does the guy's knee comes up into his groin.

His whole stomach drops. The sudden urge to vomit. He's almost definitely going to puke. He's too far away from the guy now, but he can't move. All he can do is watch as the guy rolls out his neck and smiles, blood on his teeth, and raises the gun.

Then someone yells, off to Ben's left.

"Hey! Hey *mudak*!"

It's Alyona. The guy doesn't even blink. Just points the gun toward her and Ben's barely got time to register any of this when the guy suddenly flies off in the opposite direction, like he's gotten yanked by stage cords. He flips up onto the hood of a vehicle, hitting his head on the first revolution in a way that slows him and crumples up his back and produces the unmistakable sound of something breaking that can't be righted.

It's a black SUV—it's the *Pilot,* Ben realizes. Screeched to a stop right where the guy'd been standing. There's smoke in his eyes. The stench of rubber and gas. Then his wife gets out and nods. He's too stunned to say anything back. She picks up the gun and tosses it to Ben.

"Let's go," she says. It's not until he hears her voice that he realizes it's Axel.

MARANDA

She comes to in the backseat of a car with what feels like an axe hacked into the center of her skull. Leather. The smell of body odor. Outside is a press of people wanting to shoot you or wanting to shoot *into* you.

Klara says: *Oh good, this again.*

But then someone takes her hand, which never happens, and asks, "You okay?"

She tries to open her eyes. Everything's hot. Light crams itself in.

The hole-punched things come back. Anchorage. Waiting outside the condo. The scruffy guy pulling her into the Pilot. Axel scooting himself free.

And Gracie.

Gracie.

"Where is she?" she asks, frantic. "Did you find her?"

Ben won't answer. He keeps shushing her, saying it's okay. But there are spiders in her blood. A sun in her head. As she tries to shake them out he keeps holding her arms down.

"*Stop it,*" Axel barks. His voice feels like a stick across match paper. "*She hates that.*"

Ben opens his hands and leans back. She squeezes her fists, inhales. *Calm down, bitch,* Klara says. Maranda opens her hands, exhales.

"Did you find her?" she asks, calmer now.

"Not yet," Ben says. "But we think we know where she is."

"We?"

They're moving. They're in a car and it's moving and there's someone else driving. A wifey by the looks, but Maranda doesn't know her.

"Alyona," the woman says into the mirror.

"Maranda. You…you in the life too, Alyona?"

Alyona checks the side mirror. She makes a sharp cut out of traffic. "Not anymore, bitch," she says, and laughs.

The Audi won't go past second gear. One tire's flat. But at least it's moving. Maranda blots at the cut above her eye and folds the shirt clean and blots on the other side.

"All right," she says. "We get there. We charge in, get back out."

"I don't know," Ben says. "That's…risky."

"I don't care. I'm sorry, but I don't care. Now's not the time for us to go chicken-shit. We're here to get Gracie. I'm *going* to get her."

Eventually Ben runs his tongue over his teeth and looks out the window.

Good enough, Maranda thinks.

Near the dock, the streets are on the verge of riot. Crowds press against barricades, against clusters of soldiers. The windows in every building are either plywooded over or shattered-out mouths.

Suddenly, a locomotive passes deep in the earth. The street shudders and falls. Maranda can't tell if the quake comes from the ground or her mind, but either way she wants to crawl into her head and disappear. The crowd screams. A beggar with white earmuffs and a ponytail collapses against a barricade. There are gunshots nearby. Someone climbs onto the roof of a parked car and sets to smashing it with a baseball bat.

Real, she decides.

They park, and Alyona points to the MAYA III at the other end of the docks, across a thoroughfare and a long stretch of crowd.

Everything's pressing in from the outside. Muffled screams, shattered glass. Another gunshot, maybe. Maranda can feel things dropping away. She's trying to wrest hold of herself, but then there's a sudden noise, and the car dips forward. Feet go up and over the car, leaving boot prints on the back window.

Either she screams or Alyona screams. But when she opens her eyes she's on the floor, covering her head. She can hear the voices talking inside. A few starting to yell.

Axel's going: *All right kid. Let me out.*

Guardian says: *It might be time to let one of us, Maranda.*

Other people run by, overtop the car. The beginnings of a mob.

Her heart's going to firework any second now. But she's sick of leaving, sick of running, sick of being so damn useless all the time. She's grabbing so hard at Ben's arm her skin might burst.

Axel says: *Yo. She's not letting me!*

"Hey," Ben says. She hangs on to his eyes. Out of her periphery a streetlight comes down across the road, but she wills herself not to look. Other feet bang over the roof. She closes her eyes and doesn't force anything, allows everything its place. She won't run away.

Momentarily, she's waterproof. Sounds muffle. When she opens her eyes again she can still hear the voices, but she's back in control.

Guardian says: *Okay.*

Axel says: *Fine. Have at it then.*

Outside, the crowd surges past. There's a little girl all by herself, running a few steps and looking back and stopping, then running more. She makes eye contact with Maranda, and the picture vibrates. She about stops breathing.

It's her.

Gracie.

BEN

When the door opens Ben gets a quick whiff of burn and shriek, but it slams quiet again before he even realizes Maranda's gone.

"Mar?" He tries to unbuckle but can barely get his hands to work. "Mar!"

Alyona follows him out. It's like opening the door to a wind tunnel. Crowd and mob all around. Pure noise. Cars are burning, tires melted to the road. Flames sneak from under the hoods. One explodes, lifting entirely free of the earth as a belch of smoke flowers toward the sun.

Alyona shouts, "There!"

Maranda's already way ahead of them, running directly into the current of the mob, trying to sidle her way through. She's got to be crazy. Everyone's bearing baseball bats and rebar. They're moving with a continuous, slithering noise.

Everything in him wants to turn around. There's maybe forty feet of open road between he and the crowd. He could get away if he wanted to. But instead he shakes his head and sprints forward. The mob hits him—or he the mob—like the slap of a wave. He actually loses his breath. He ducks his shoulders. Someone spits on him. He honestly can't tell if he's getting forward at all.

Another explosion. A burning tire steers down the road. A guy laughs, kicks it onward.

"Mar! Maranda!"

There's another, different-sounding explosion. He feels an air-pulse pass his ear, then hit heavy and wet behind him. It's not until the screams start that he realizes it was a bullet.

There's another shot. He ducks. Another and another. They sound like fireworks. The air's full of screaming, the knotted crowd coming undone. He sees what looks like Maranda's sleeve get sucked into an alleyway, fast as a bird. It's her. It's got to be her.

Alyona, he remembers. He turns and she's behind him, giving a short fight through the crowd, but then gives up and runs with the tide. She waves him on, but he's got no chance of reaching her anyway. There's no choice. He heads for the alley, sprinting blindly at a half-crouch, arms over his head, until he stumbles into the sudden quiet.

He has to lean forward to catch his breath, holding his knees. God, his heart. Maranda's facing away, on her knees. She's talking. She keeps saying the same thing over and over.

"Gracie," she's saying. "It's me. Gracie, it's *me*."

MARANDA

It's her. It's actually her.

Gracie's right here, within arm's reach.

Everything's going to be okay. It's going to be okay.

The world's packed in gauze. Nothing but Gracie is real. It had been too loud on the streets, deafening. That's why Gracie wouldn't stop running. But now, out of the noise, Maranda can hear the echo of her own footsteps. Her breath rebounding off brick. Gracie's got her back to her, shaking. Her little shape makes a throb in the air.

"Gracie," Maranda says. "It's me. It's Maranda."

When Gracie finally turns around, a gulf opens up in Maranda's chest. She has to fight the urge to look away.

Look what they've done to her.

Gracie's eyes are dark and smear-painted. Her little eyebrows perfect arches. There's a fire-anger in her face—it hits Maranda like a thrown car battery.

They're too late. It's already starting.

Maranda clenches back a gasp. She's falling away from herself piece by piece. Not her alters. It's like her actual body is earthquake-broken.

"I don't know you," Gracie spits, balling her fists. Maranda sees she's wearing a half-dozen cheap little rings. "What the hell you want with me?"

"Gracie, it's me. It's Maranda."

"I don't know you."

"Gracie, Gracie. It's me. It's Maranda."

Inside, Axel says: *Oh shit.*

Klara sighs.

Gracie's confused, that's all. She's angry. She's so small, god she's small, and she's traumatized. But everything's going to be okay.

When Maranda reaches out to take her wrist, Gracie turns to cut wire. She shudders, writhing in Maranda's hand, her little arm no more than bird-bone.

"Get off me! Hey, no!"

Maranda grabs harder. "Gracie, it's me. It's me!"

"Stop it! Don't hurt me. Don't take me."

"Gracie, we came to get you. It's me, it's Maranda."

Suddenly, Ben's behind her. He's grabbing her, yelling, "Mar, what are you *doing?*" but she can barely hear him.

"Don't take me! Don't take me!"

Soon Maranda's yelling too. She's saying Gracie's name over and over, like it will shatter the spell in her mind. When Gracie hits at her arms Maranda, just for a second, holds them down, and Gracie jumps, starts running in place, flickering. She's got wild terror in her eyes. She wrests herself backward, but Maranda doesn't let go. Ben's arms are around her waist, and he's pulling at her, yelling her name.

"Maranda! What the hell are you doing? What are you talking about?"

She's losing her grip. She hears somebody inside. The cold voice. Laughing.

BEN

It's like Maranda's seizing. Stepped on electric fire. It's pushed him right past fear into anger. She's scaring the shit out of him.

There's nobody here. Maranda's talking to herself, wrestling thin air.

She keeps saying, "It's me, it's me, it's me" but there's nobody there.

He grabs her around the waist—tries to shake her out of it—but still she won't stop. He's yelling almost to the point of tears.

"What the hell are you doing? What are you talking about?"

She tries to peel his arms from her waist, then starts battering them with her fists. She kicks backward at his knees. Finally, she stops hitting him and slumps forward, howling Gracie's name over and over and over. When he lets go she collapses.

"Mar, what the hell? What the *hell*?"

She sobs, a moan that'll split her in half. "Why wouldn't she come with me? Why wouldn't she come with me?"

He looks behind them. The tail of the mob is still running past the mouth of the alley. Someone with an actual torch. They're standing on shatter. There's a maw opening up underneath.

He's almost too afraid to ask: "Who are you talking about?"

She wipes her nose and blinks at him. "What?"

"Who? Who are you talking about? Who were you talking to?"

Her voice goes quiet. "I came back for her. She knows who I am."

Oh God.

No. Not this.

They should have stayed in Juneau. The ground opens. He feels their small foundation rumbling. Sheaves of rock breaking away. It's going to swallow them both.

He tries to keep his voice calm but firm. "We have to get out of here, Mar."

"She knows me."

"Can we…we need to go. Let's talk about this later."

Now she looks right at him, and her eyes blaze. His heart falls away.

"So that's it? You just give up. Like a little…"

"Mar—"

"Not as easy as Ben wants it to be, no problem. He's got other options. Hey, you should pay someone to get her. Maybe that?"

"Mar, come on."

"Maybe if—"

"Mar!"

"Don't *fucking* interrupt me! You were the one freaking her out, and I'm here trying to keep her from getting fucked by creeps like *you*!"

"Goddamnit Mar, listen to yourself!"

Maranda stops. She twists her head to the side.

"You're *crazy*," Ben groans, pushing at his eyes. "There's nobody here."

Maranda's voice, when she speaks again, is small and quiet. "What?"

"Gracie's. Not. Real."

MARANDA

Not this. Anything but this.

It's going to devour her.

Maybe she mis-heard. Maybe Ben will take it back, change his mind. Or maybe, seeing her, maybe he'll lie and say he *did* see Gracie, even though he didn't.

Yes, she thinks. Yes. Do that.

Where'd she go? Where did Gracie go?

Farther down in the alley is a puddle of lemon-yellow, a dumpster, a wooden fence. There's no sign of any girl.

Her life's a blender. Lid off. Gracie's dripping from the ceiling. She hears someone laughing. Just laughing and laughing and laughing.

She's nuts, isn't she? This is how crazy dies.

The cold voice says: *It's kind of a relief, ain't it? It's easier, not to fight so hard.*

Did *she* think that, or did she overhear it?

Listen to yourself. The hell does it matter?

For a second, Gracie's standing in front of her, surrounded by a pulsing aura. She expands and contracts in the air, shrinks all the way down to a single, luminescent point. Then she starts getting bigger and bigger, until she takes up everything, until she's everywhere, so big you see right through her, and disappears.

Maranda's falling. Tiles are falling out of mid-air. Behind each one is a void that's going to suck her right in. There's a wind snap-pulling at her clothes, furious and black and alive. She tries but she can't move away. She's sliding. Her feet are scraping over the road.

BEN

As soon as the switch starts, he can tell it's different.

Maranda groans, wincing. She presses the heel of a palm into her eye. An earthquake she's trying to hold inside. She cracks her neck one way, then the other. She rolls her shoulders and the motion goes all the way down her arms, into her fingers and legs, like she's pulling on a suit of skin.

Then, just as suddenly, it's over. She looks right at him.

He tries to keep his voice even. "Who's this?"

She gives a thin smile. Her voice is throaty, chilled slow. "She's a pain in the ass, isn't she? You both are."

"Gracie, she's…"

She waves off the question. "Innocence, whatever. The stuff that got fucked up."

"She's an alter?"

She lifts her eyebrows. "Get the man a prize."

Ben wipes his hands on his thighs. He reaches for something to say and comes up short. Lightning's jumping his capillaries.

"Easy soldier," she says. "You look like you're gonna hyperventilate."

"So what now? What's happening?"

She laughs and turns around, marching out of the alleyway. Ben follows.

Out on the street, the noise hits him like an open hand. He'd forgotten. Half the cars are smashed and burning. The street is jeweled with glass. Maranda—*whoever* this is—walks like she doesn't even notice, purpose and muscle in every step. Ben's at a jog to keep up.

"This just isn't going to work," she says. "Maranda can't handle it out here. Thanks for your help, but…we're going back."

People run by them on both sides. Ben realizes she's heading for the docks.

"Where's Maranda?"

"I'm afraid she's not here right now. Please, you know, leave a message after the beep."

"Just let me talk to—"

She pivots, gets right in his face. "BEEP!" It breaks her into a genuine belly-laugh.

"When is she coming back?"

"She's not. *I'm* in charge now. About time someone with half a brain ran this shitshow." She lifts the hem of Maranda's shirt with two fingers, disgust on her face. "The hell does she have us wearing?"

The riot is a storm around them. Smell of gas everywhere. The carrier's close and enormous. The letters MAYA III look razored into the orange paint.

Ben's throat feels an inch small. "Who are you?"

She smiles like she's been waiting for this. "I'm Hagar."

"What do you *do,* Hagar?"

"Look at you, trying to make nice. You wanna know what I do?"

Everything's falling away. They're on the precipice of total fuck-dom.

"Yeah."

"You sure?"

"Yes."

She leans in close, whispering. "I give Maranda what she deserves."

All Ben's fight goes away. He's tried and he's tried, but he lost. That's it.

Hagar holds her hands out like she's just presented the reveal of a magic trick. "She's a whore, Ben. That's all."

With that, she turns and jogs up the ramp.

MARANDA

Maranda can't see anything. She's deep inside. She just hears the voice, the cold one, coming from every direction.

Look at the sky. Same color as a slit wrist. How much time you think anyone's got?

Maranda doesn't have the strength to resist. The voice keeps on.

No more running. No more waiting. This is all you are.

BEN

It's like he's not even there. Like this is happening to someone else and he's only watching.

Nearby, a soldier fires into the sky. Someone throws a Molotov cocktail from a window and it lights with a *whoosh*, spilling over the pavement.

On the other side of all this, he watches Hagar jog up the ramp. He keeps waiting for her to look back, imagining that she'll turn and see the look on his face, that she or Maranda or, hell, *any* of them, will think better of it and come back, say they're sorry, say it was a joke, or just run into his arms and say nothing at all.

But she doesn't look back, not once.

Police with riot shields push against the mob. Mayhem seeps from the cracks. The world is suffused with pulsing color. There are so many red and blue cruiser lights you can't even tell where they're coming from.

He's got no idea how much time passes. Eventually he's back at the Audi. It's covered over with shoe prints. The back windshield's gone. One of the headlights is smashed and dangling by a wire. He gets in and sits down—it's all he can think to do. Everything feels obscenely close, and at the same time very far away.

The street's abandoned, the mob further down the docks. The pavement is littered with glass and refuse. There's a pair of shoes in the middle of the road. A small pool of what's either oil or blood.

Eventually, a few pickers emerge from the alleys, start kicking over rubble, nudging rafters with a toe. A boy sits in the street and tries on one of the shoes. Just a few days and you'll do anything.

Ben notices a girl in pumps and a red tank top lean against one of the light poles. She has one leg jutted out. It's not a conscious thought, not really, but he feels in his belly an impulse that goes: My God, wouldn't *that* be nice?

Even now, after everything they've gone through, there's still that part of him. He lets his head fall. Jesus.

It's only fair Maranda left. There's got to be a point where things can't be fixed, or where trying to fix them would just be worse for the other person. She's not going to come back. The certainty of this settles over him, weighty and substantial. Enough is enough, he thinks.

He could stay here, camp in Anchorage and wait for whatever's going to happen, or he could drive out of the city, just drive and drive. There's not much else to do. Either way, the world will still end in fire and he in silence.

He closes the door and reaches for the knapsack. At the top is his father's New Testament, heavy as hell despite its slender binding. It flips open to the note scrawled across the front page. Ben doesn't even read it, simply closes his hand and rips. Something in him gives a very loud *yes*. He tosses the book into the backseat, where Chipmunk's Calico rabbit is lying face up, forgotten.

He gets out of the car because he has to, because he can't breathe. But as soon as he does he realizes, weirdly, that he knows exactly what to do.

He can hear his heart in his ears. The girl's still standing there, at the end of the alleyway, but this time he ignores whatever beast in clamoring in his belly and hands her a water bottle. Her forehead wrinkles, and she looks up at him. Her lips are chapped. She's got bags under her eyes.

Just a kid, Ben realizes. He'd like to tell her something but he doesn't have anything to say. He gives a dumb nod and keeps on.

He's jumpy. He puts up his hood and buries his hands in his pockets. God, his chest is hammering.

Up ahead he can read the name of the ship in black stencil: MAYA III.

"Okay," he says out loud. "Okay."

The bowels and industrial innards of the cargo ship. A guy pats Ben down, takes his gun, then waves him down a long straightaway with doors on either side, enormous pipes running overhead. There's the heavy drum of machinery everywhere. Pistons firing endlessly.

A few other guys are lurking about. Other johns. Ben tries to look like any of them, too skittishly horny to hold eye contact. He keeps his hands in his pockets and his hood up. He's embarrassed by how easily this comes, how practiced he is, but tries not to think about that.

A girl stumbles out of a room. She stands there, blinking, until a guy grabs her by the bicep and pulls her back, kicks the door shut. Ben keeps walking. There's a girl with a john at the end of the hall and when she raises her voice the guy backhands her, then gets immediately sucker punched by a burly dude in a black t-shirt who comes out of nowhere and begins to drag-escort the bleeding guy away.

Finally, he sees Maranda. Down at the far end of the hall. He can tell by the first step she takes, the way she holds her head on her shoulders, that it's still Hagar.

A guy in denim walks with her. As Ben watches, the guy moves his hand from her ass and tries two keys before getting a door unlocked and ushering her in. They're only forty, maybe fifty feet away.

"I'll tell him you're here," the guy says, leaving the door ajar and walking in Ben's direction. He holds his breath. Trying to stall, to look natural, he glances idly into a room and sees a girl spread-eagled, naked from the waist down, passed out or asleep.

The guy's right there before Ben can look away. "You cool?" he laughs.

"Yeah, yeah," Ben coughs. He's starting to sweat. Thankfully the guy shakes his head and keeps walking.

Jesus, his pulse is going in his temples. He rubs his face and wipes his palms on his jeans. Okay, he breathes. Go.

Ben walks past the door. He turns around to scope the hallway again. There's only a few people. When a patron gets overly handsy and the one remaining guard steps in, Ben casually slips into the room.

MARANDA

In her head, she's going faster than free-fall.

It's black as fuck, nothing but a wind—a great howling suck, and a hand around her ankle pulling her down, down, down.

It sounds like a freight train. Like a tornado. Her brain's an F5. If you could see anything in there, you'd see cars in trees stripped of their bark. Houses all rubble and sticks.

She hears a girl sob-screaming and recognizes the sound of it. It's herself—it's her own memories down here.

Hagar's taking her right into the heart of the past.

The sounds are getting closer. There's a train light funneling down the tracks.

BEN

When he locks the door behind him Hagar props herself up on an elbow, cocks a hip. It's a small room. An unplugged mini-fridge and a blue couch and a mounted rack of antlers on the floor. A baffling print of a clown made entirely of vegetables.

Hagar lifts an eyebrow and opens her mouth just enough so he can see her tongue behind her teeth.

"Fine," she sighs.

"What?" For a second he thinks this means she'll come with him.

"We can screw—once. Before she gets back in the game. No charge. You better hurry though. Not that that's usually a problem."

"Where's Maranda?"

Hagar looks at her nails.

"Let me talk to her."

He watches for an eye flick, a crack of the neck, but there's nothing. She continues examining her hands. Then slowly—*God,* so slowly—she looks up at him.

Something's wrong. "You can't do this," Ben says. His throat's getting tight. "I want to talk to her. Maranda. You have to let me talk to her. You don't have the...you can't do this."

"Oh I promise, I can. She had her turn. Now it's mine."

"Let me talk to Maranda."

"She's…indisposed."

"Guardian then."

She winces, he's pretty sure. Just a little bit of an eye-twitch.

"Come on, man," she says.

"Let me talk to Guardian."

A new nastiness comes out. She shakes her head, trying to thrash herself present. But her voice, when she speaks, is definitely fading.

"Can't we just…fuck and…leave it alone?"

She digs her fingernails into her arm. Almost enough to draw blood.

He tries to be firm, even though anxiety is all but leaking from his skin. "Guardian. Let me talk to Guardian."

Hagar closes her eyes. She flinches. He watches the shape of her mouth change, and a few seconds later she opens her eyes, calm. Ben lets out a breath he hasn't even realized he's been holding. It's Guardian, thank God. Everything's going to be okay.

Two jets scream across the sky. The whole room rattles—you can feel it in your teeth. Out the small porthole, people duck and cover.

Guardian's voice is urgent, sharp. "Where's Maranda?"

Ben tightens. "What do you mean?"

"I can't feel her. I can't find Maranda. She's not there."

A muffled boom shakes the world. Ben half-ducks, one arm lifted to his head. You can feel the fraying of every tether. The sudden possibility that everything is going to come apart.

"What does that mean?"

"I have to go inside, to ask some questions," Guardian says. "I'm going to send Chipmunk out."

"*Chipmunk*?"

Guardian nods. "Yes. She's…strong. More than you think. But you need to keep her distracted. I don't want Hagar coming back."

Ben starts to say something, but Guardian's already gone.

MARANDA

All around, wind screams. It blows her hair. Tears skin right off of her skull. Maggot-burrows into her brain.

She's at the bottom of a long darkness. An inner well. Already, she's forgetting what outside even means.

The cold voice says: *You've been running away, but this is all that there is.*

Heat's pounding off her in waves. Fire-mist on her skin. All around her are walls of water. It's dark, blood-black. Got to be 200 degrees. There are shapes and colors on each of the waterfalls. Pictures moving. In one of them there's someone naked, but that's all she sees before she slams her eyes shut again.

Look, bitch. This is what's real. You're living in a fantasy.

If she looks she'll shatter. Her cobbled-together brain will explode. She'll wash away piece by piece.

Maranda's gritting her teeth so hard she's shaking. All the while the voice is just laughing at her. Laughing and laughing and laughing.

BEN

When Chipmunk finishes switching into Maranda's body, she screws her face into a pout, staring at the floor. She's breathing raggedly, sniffling, holding her forearm to her chest like it's a wounded bird.

Jesus, how do you fix anything this broken?

"Hey," he says. "Hey…"

Another *boom.* Muffled yells through the window. Chipmunk covers her ears.

"Hey, look here," Ben says. He has to say it twice before she looks up, though he still has no idea what he's supposed to do. "That hurt?" he asks, nodding at her arm.

Chipmunk studies him. She looks back and forth from his eyes to his hands.

"Want a robot arm?" When she doesn't answer he holds up a hand. "Won't hurt, promise."

Slowly, she nods. Ben takes her hand and turns it over. She's not wearing her ring anymore. The hand is both a woman's and a child's at once. Sliding her sleeve up to the elbow, he runs his eyes over a raised ladder of scars. Chipmunk watches.

"Ready?"

Ben flattens his hand and lowers it against her elbow, making chainsaw noises. She flinches.

"Easy," he says.

He mimes taking the old arm and tosses it across the room, making a *clunk* sound as it lands. He fits on a new one, twisting and pushing until it clicks into place.

Outside, artillery falls. Enormous and rhythmic. All you can see through the porthole is a sky that looks rusted, scudding planes of smoke. Chipmunk glances up.

"Where's Gracie?" she asks. "Why isn't Gracie here?"

"Look here," Ben says. "You ready?"

He pretends to drill five screws around the thickest part of her forearm, then blowtorches the two pieces together and buffs out the rough spots.

There's a louder, more immediate explosion. The ship vibrates. The lights in the room flicker and go out. People outside are screaming. He has to force himself not to look too. If he even glances outside, he knows she'll do the same, and then maybe get scared and sputter out, and who knows who might come in to take her place?

"What color should it be?" he asks. "Pink? Purple?"

She bites her lip, nodding yes for purple. Ben counts across a shelf of imaginary paint cans, takes one and starts shaking it.

"Black it is…" he says.

"No!" Chipmunk laughs, pulling back her arm.

Ben frowns. "Not black?"

"Purple!"

"Shoot, that's right."

He picks another to spray over it, then leans back to let her inspect the new limb.

"That better?"

She moves it around, looking at it from both sides, wiggling her fingers and wrist. "It looks just like the old one."

"Sure does," Ben says. "You were brave."

He can tell she's getting foggy. She keeps closing her eyes.

"I think," she starts, her voice slurry and low. "Guardian…I think I gotta go."

Everything's suffused in copper tang. The lights flicker and come back on again. Outside, someone's firing shots into the air and every once in a while he can hear the high thin scream of a plane. Ben wipes his mouth. He forces himself to breathe.

She has her eyes closed, keeps squeezing them. When she finally opens them again, he can tell right away it's Guardian.

"Well?"

"Two are missing," Guardian says.

"What does that mean?"

"Hagar is trying to run things. She put Maranda in the Cell."

"The Cell?"

Guardian gives Ben a look, then turns away.

"Guardian. What's the Cell?"

"It's bad, Ben. The things I don't want her remembering go there. The worst ones."

The room's too small. The ship quakes again, a deep thrumming in the water. A runnel of dust falls from the ceiling.

"So, what?" Ben says. "What do we do?"

"I don't know."

"You *don't know?*"

"It's a vault, Ben. It's supposed to keep things *in.*"

"She's in there right now?"

"Yes."

It strikes him, weirdly, that he has never understood anything about hell until this exact moment. That *this*—his wife's own mind—is the deepest circle. He wants to run, honestly. He wants to run away. But even if he does he'll still know it, that Maranda's locked in her own head, watching it all again and again. He'll never be able to *not* know it.

Guardian's watching him, turning him end over end.

"I need to know you're serious about Maranda," Guardian says. "What about the other girls?"

"What about them?"

"Any you'd do this for?"

"No."

"We could find another host, someone else to take her place. *I* can host. We send alter after alter out. No one will ever know."

"Leave her in there?"

"Klara, maybe. She'd be easier. You wouldn't have to deal with…everything the two of you are dealing with."

"No. I can't…I won't leave her in there."

Guardian nods. "Okay. I'll go. This will probably be—she's going to be reliving some of her worst memories, Ben."

Ben swallows. "What do I need to do?"

"Let it happen. Trust me. And if I don't make it back out…"

Ben waits, holding eye contact.

"Don't you dare fuck with her anymore."

Guardian's eyes close, and Ben forces himself to breathe. He smells heat. The light in the window is a steely orange. Screams melt through the hull. Nearby, in the ship, a woman is crying.

"Well well well!" a voice yells from the hallway. Ben knows who it is immediately, somehow. Luke.

Maranda's body is lying on the bed, palms to the ceiling. Guardian seems to bubble up to the surface, fuzzy sounding and distant but nevertheless *there*.

"Don't…don't let him near her."

Ben does another scan of the room. His gun's gone. There's nothing here in the way of a weapon. Time slows. Everything is lit by spilling firelight. The hum of florescence. He sees the first waves of pain wash onto Maranda's face, deep in a dream. Luke is just outside the door. In a single motion, Ben steps on the wooden mount and wrenches off one of the antlers. A small moan escapes Maranda's lips. Her forehead wrinkles.

A key enters the lock and turns. Ben raises the antler. The door opens.

MARANDA

Maranda's curled into a ball, covering her face. It's so hot you can't draw a full breath. She tries and tries, but she can't. It feels like she'll never move again.

Hagar called this the Cell. Maranda could see her. Only for a second. She was laughing, laughing.

All around, memories are projected onto the spray, all warbly and ghost. If she looks it's going to undo her. It'll force her down to where she'll never come back out.

She can hear the voices. All of them.

Dad threw her bear away. He said she had a nosebleed but she didn't. He did something bad, worse than a spanking. Everything hurts. Every time she touches her lip she gets blood on her hands. Gracie says not to be scared but she's scared. Her bear had a lot of blood on it so he threw it away.

Sitting in the smoke-clouds of a bar. Waiting for men to buy you a drink. Untouchable. The more untouchable you look the more they pay to touch you. This is the way to hold a cigarette. Maximum, how do you say, seductiveness. You hold it between your two fingers, then against your mouth. Yes? It looks like a gesture of, you could say, sexual things. So the boys think that. They think you mean sexual things.

On one of the walls there's blood on the inside of her knee. Jesus. That's all she can see. Chicken legs. A trickle of blood. She's so small.

No. She can't look anymore. She won't.

Luke and the other fucker tied her to a chair. Who does that? Could've gotten out. But then the other guy comes up with a needle. That's a pussy move, man. She could've gotten out.

It's dark. Crushingly dark. She's tired of resisting. It's easier to just give in.

There's another memory projected on the water-wall. The back of a truck. It's dark, other girls nearby. Someone's vomited. There are pinpricks of light all around. She's flying through empty space, nothing to keep her bearings, but when the truck stops you just want it to keep going. You know what stopping means.

The floor is carpeted in that hard, coarse kind that rubs your skin raw. The beginnings of rug-burn on your knees already. It's better to let it happen. Easier and quicker. You give in and you do not fight and you look for the void in your mind, the room you can enter and hide. You hear him laboring behind you and feel nothing.

She's tied to a chair. So tight her feet seem to be filling with dark. It looks like it's just the two of them, Luke and Maranda, but she can feel someone else there, outside the circle of light. Every once in a while whoever it is coughs or scuffs his shoe.

Luke claps his hands clean and looks at her. You can see, in his eyes, what he thinks about her. The slut. Like he'd feel bad for her if she wasn't so easy to hate.

The other guy steps in. He's wearing cargo shorts and a coat, carrying a red toolbox.

No. She can't watch. Not that one.

On another wall Klara is still smoking. A hand comes in from the side and starts squeezing her breast. She doesn't even react. Just lets it go. Takes her cigarette and looks at it and then puts it back and keeps going. Releases two streams of vapor, one from each nostril.

Have you seen her bear? Her dad threw her bear away. He threw it away. He said she had a nosebleed but she didn't. It's bad to pick your nose so she doesn't do it. Sometimes Gracie does when she can't help it. But he made her do the other thing. Like a spanking only worse. Then the bear was covered in blood and it was her fault so he threw it away. It must be lower down in the trash. But he can't breathe down there, not with all this on top of him. She tells him she's coming but he can't hear, he can't breathe. Standing hurts. She has to sit down. She has wet on herself, but she doesn't remember peeing. There's a pizza box and cans that are crushed and then a big warm gloop over everything. It gets on her hands and when she smells it she gets sick and now there is more of the gloop, and it is hot and her stomach hurts and her mouth tastes bad. But her bear is under there and he can't breathe. He can't breathe.

When the cords finally snap good lord it feels good in Axel's shoulders. There's a circle of bleeding fire around his wrists but it's a matter of will and now they're free, but by the time he tilts himself back in the chair to get his ankles they're moving in already. The shorts guy is jamming a needle into his goddamn arm.

When the screen parts and someone splashes half into the Cell Maranda thinks it's another memory. That she is finally, thankfully, losing her mind.

"Maranda," the person says, and she looks up. They're standing in the water, the spray scalding and hissing. Even hunched over they're twice her height. Gray and thin, like you took a person and stretched them out. All bone, no weakness. No gender-marker to speak of.

It's Guardian, she realizes. Knows it instinctively. Guardian winces and indicates the screen behind her. "Look," Guardian says. "Look."

"I can't."

"It's the only way out of here."

"It's too much."

"Maranda, it already happened."

She's crying now. Panic is shot-loose through her body. Guardian groans, standing up straighter. She can see curls of steam lifting from the rimpled skin.

"You have to look. If you don't look you're never going to get out of here."

Behind Guardian, there are others. A whole crowd of them. Some she recognizes, some she can barely see in the dark. Chipmunk with her rabbit, Axel in a leather coat. Klara's smoking a cigarette and tugging at the hem of her skirt.

"You have us," Guardian says. "We're here."

Slowly, everything goes quiet. The Cell starts to shift and change. She forces herself to turn toward the screen.

BEN

As soon as the door opens, Ben charges. Shoulder to stomach, he hits Luke with all the force he can muster and feels Luke's wind go out in a soundless moan.

Ben scrambles back to his feet and hoists the antler, stagger-stepping, but Luke catches the swing and forces Ben's arm back. He's stronger than Ben expected.

He feels a foot go around his leg. Luke's face swings up, large, and there's a thunderclap of white and they're both on the ground again, tangled. Ben sees, as if in slow motion, that Luke's holding a gun. Ben grabs his wrist and bites, hard as he can, until he tastes blood and feels the flesh give, and the gun falls and gets kicked away as Luke stands, pulling a knife from his belt.

The antler hisses as it cuts the air. Ben's all fury, but Luke smiles as he parries each blow with his fist, the knife. There could have been, in some not-so-alternate timeline, kinship between the two of them, Ben thinks. They're not entirely unalike.

Luke lunges, but it's a feint, and as Ben sidesteps the knife flashes in the flickering hall-light and he can feel the air of it on his cheek. He stumbles, claps a hand to his face but there's no cut, no blood.

Maranda's sobbing nearby. Luke sneers.

A distance looms up in Ben, a disregard. He realizes, all at once, that he doesn't have a chance, that he's going to die here, but it doesn't affect him the way he thought it would. He's just buying time while Guardian gets Maranda out.

As Luke swings harder—broad, crazed arcs—Ben allows himself to be backed into a stairwell. It's filled with an enormous, echoing hum. Ben swings and Luke's block smoothly becomes an elbow to the face. By the time he can see again the knife is animate and conscious, intent on burying itself in his abdomen. He sucks himself up out of the way, stumbles down several stairs. Luke's no longer smiling. There's a sound from deep underneath them like thunder and everything begins to vibrate and move. Luke takes hold of the railing, but Ben falls all the way to the next landing.

The earthquake keeps going. Ben tries to get up, but his body won't obey. Fuck, fuck. The steel floor is so close he can see the striations. Finally, he lifts himself by the railing and when he turns around Luke is there, standing like he's been waiting the entire time. Ben can smell him, which is weird. Sweat and too much cologne. Ben twists, stupidly trying to get away, and at the same time Luke moves his hand.

He feels the knife enter his shoulder. It's cold. Ben has time to think that it seems, if not gentle, then at least done without rancor. It just happens. There's a scrape, steel on bone, which goes all the way down his arm, and then the coldness goes away, replaced by warmth and the weight of blood in his clothes.

Another earthquake. Things pick up and set back where they were. Ben doesn't remember falling but he's on the floor. He's all the way down at the bottom of the stairs. He tries to move his arm and a sharpness goes all the way down to his feet. He hears someone scream *Fuck!* and realizes it's him. It sounds like he's underwater. Things are slowing down. He can't tell the thrum of the engines from the thrum of his head but they're both ponderous, untrustworthy.

MARANDA

In place of the Cell is the double-wide where she grew up. She's six again. Right away she can recognize the Calico rabbit. Little Maranda making it play-run across a bed. She watches herself get up to go into the kitchen for a drink.

In the living room is her father. He's wiry, poorly kempt. Lying on a stained couch in a sprawl of beer cans. The TV is blurry with underwater shapes.

It's porn, her now-self realizes.

It takes him a while to notice she's there, but when he does he lurches upright, grabbing the back of the couch. The way he does it seems supernatural, the way a vampire would rise from a coffin.

He's yelling before he's even stood. "Hey! Don't look at that! Only dirty girls watch that kinda thing! Dirty girls!"

It echoes. *Dirty girls dirty girls dirty girls.*

Suddenly, he's dragging her by the bicep down a hall. She knows what's next, she's used to it. The belt, bent over the toilet. But as they pass the bathroom, she feels a new fury emanating from him.

"Course," he mutters, "you always been a bad girl."

Maranda blinks. She's in two places at once now. There and here. She's pinned to her bed. He smells like beer.

The pain that comes next—even in memory—is the sun. It's nuclear, big as god. You try to close your eyes but it doesn't leave—you see your fingerbones through your eyelids. Her skin sizzles away, she's all meat.

Pain digs out the top of her fucking head, like forcing a coke can into the end of a lemon. Everything rearranges and pushes out her eyes. She's a blender, lid off. Guts are going to drip from the ceiling. She's face first in her own vomit, pulling at the sheets but it's not getting her anywhere.

Finally he steps back, breathing hard. Zips himself.

Pain heartbeats in her skull. There are fingernail marks in the wall.

He sighs, spits.

"You're nothing," he says.

She wants to go away. To sink down and down and down. But Guardian lays a hand on her shoulder. "Look. Keep looking."

For a while, she just lies on her little pillow, staring at the Calico rabbit. Her hair's messy with vomit. When she tries to stand she falls instantaneously, like she's been shot.

But then she starts moving again. She braces her hands against the floor, gets her feet under her, and slowly— incredibly—gets up.

Guardian's standing with all the others behind. They're all watching her.

Guardian holds out a hand.

She takes it, gets helped to her feet. Together, watching her, they all move in and hold back the water with their bodies. It feels like she is just now meeting people she's written letters to her entire life. She can smell flesh steaming, but none of them move until she's safely out.

Maranda opens her eyes to flickering light through the window. The sound of distant screaming. Where's Ben? Where's Gracie? The last she remembers they were all in an alleyway, but how long ago was that? It feels like she's been out for days.

She tries to focus. Puts a fist around her heart and finds it solid. Like a baseball.

Get up, she tells herself.

Everything tumbles. She makes her way slow across the room, surface to surface. Her hands bounce and shake. She doesn't recognize the room, which is the only way she's sure she's no longer in the Cell. The past will try to kill you anytime it wants. There's a blue couch and a mini-fridge. Some weird-ass clown painting in the corner.

She stops. There's a gun looking up at her from the floor.

When she picks it up it's heavy, still warm. Enough power to rip through anything. She's turning it over in her hands when she looks up and finds Louise three feet away.

Yeah, the past will try to kill you anytime it wants.

Everything crowds in, fuzzy. A circle of black forms around her vision.

Louise makes a sad-smile, like all of this is very unfortunate. She closes the door behind her, even turns her back to make sure it shuts quietly.

Outside, there's an explosion. Maranda's eyes vibrate.

Louise licks her lips, her voice church-quiet. "I'm so happy to see you again."

Inside, Axel says: *Shoot the bitch.*

Maranda watches her hand lift the gun. Her arm wobbles and shakes.

At the same time Chipmunk says: *Mommy.*

"You look well," Louise says. "Beautiful as ever."

Maranda can barely hear. The black part of the circle is closing in.

"I hoped you'd come back. I worried about you, dear."

Maranda hesitates. Her voices—her people—she can feel them all watching in her head.

Louise opens her hands. "People are always going to need this. Why don't you come back? Be more of a supervisor. A partner."

At the end of Maranda's arm, the gun drops a little bit, but Louise doesn't even look at it. She talks very calm and very quiet.

Maybe it's easier not to fight anymore. Maranda's got no fight left.

"Of course, you could work if you want it, but you don't have to. There's safety together. Power."

A gauze over everything. As soon as she focuses on something it goes slippery and opaque. There are a number of things pressing in on her head and threatening to take over. She sees flashes of other places like lightning-bursts. A couch strewn with beer cans. Her childhood bed, blood-smeared and stripped of its sheets. A basement. The back of a truck. Flash. Flash. Flash.

In her left arm is something heavy—the gun, yes, the gun—that she just wants to drop. Louise is talking. Moving her hands. Her fingers are beautiful with rings.

This is her life. *The* life. Outside has been nothing but awful. On her own Maranda has no idea what to do.

Everything starts to go vapory again. Louise frowns, tipping her head. "Are you alright, dear?"

It's like she's riding in her own mind. She can see what her eyes would normally see, and can feel her lips forming the words, but it's requiring no volition of her own.

"Look," she hears herself say, but it's Guardian's voice saying it. "Does she look all right?"

Louise gives a little downturn of the mouth at the word "she."

"This," Guardian says, "is why you don't fuck kids."

Maranda wonders if she might be able to reach out and cause something right now. She tries to make her arm move and look—there it goes.

All of a sudden, she's out again. Her head's a windless expanse of sand. She can see for miles.

In her hand is the gun.

Maranda sees Louise see it now, really see it, noticeably dipping and raising her head to follow the bore of the pistol.

"Fuck you," Maranda says.

There's no transition. A flat bang and the wall behind Louise is suddenly decorated in splatter. Her head snaps back and one arm jerks up at the elbow. Then she's down, dark blood pooling over the floor.

Maranda watches, calm. There's still no wind across the landscape of her mind.

BEN

Ben touches the ground, leaving a handprint of blood. He's still holding the chipped-up antler, but he's in and out, and his right arm is entirely numb.

He grabs at the handrail and tries to stand. Luke is only a step or two away, shaking dust out of his hair, still holding the knife.

"Well," Luke says, flipping it around. "You tried."

He steps down and grabs Ben by the hair. Ben can't even move to fight it. He hears the buzz of the lights, watches the tiny flickerings they give off when, above them, the door bangs open, and someone points a gun.

Fuck, Ben thinks. He closes his eyes, waits. It's all he's got the strength and wherewithal to do.

Luke drops him. Ben flinches away and the gun fires twice, close and enormous, and it's only when nothing hits, and he hears the thing click empty that Ben opens his eyes to see who it is.

MARANDA

Everything in the stairwell is fire and dust.

"Well," she hears a guy say. "You tried."

His voice enters her brain like an ice pick. Luke.

There, on the landing, maybe twenty feet down, two tangled shapes are wrestling in the rubble. Ben makes a wet gasping noise as Luke pulls his head back.

There's no time. She fires blind. The gun recoils all the way through her arms. The stairwell seizures open, and she can see the bullets spark-ping off the metal. She keeps on pulling the trigger but nothing happens.

No.

Luke drops Ben, who's not moving, and starts up the stairs three at a time.

"Well well," he laughs. He knuckles blood away from his lip. Her brain goes fuzzy. An opening drain threatens to take what's left of her away.

"Look at me," Luke says, and she hears herself whine. He grabs her face with the knife hand, leans in. "For the first time in your life, you're about to be truly fucked."

She's not even thinking—her body just reacts. Luke pushes closer and at the same time she punches with her forehead, a blinding pain down her nose neither of them are expecting. Luke stumbles, just a step, but as he does she grabs his arm and pushes the knife up to his face, bearing down against his bottom lip. Luke gasps, tries to scream without moving his mouth and then there's a definite crunch. Warmth coats her fingers. She pushes harder and Luke falls backward, sliding free, into Ben who's suddenly there, who's got his arm back, ready to swing.

BEN

She hits him good. It's thick, echoes. Then—

Christ.

Luke spins, dazed, a blood-worm peeking from his nostril, his ruined bottom lip exposing a grimace of teeth. There's genuine shock in his eyes.

Ben swings the antler with his left. It's awkward but he gives it everything he's got, kind of lurching his body for leverage. Luke's eyes go to the antler without shock or fear, just as you would register the presence of anything, totally non-judgmental. He doesn't have time to lift his hands or move at all as the bulk of the antler gets him in the throat. Ben can feel all through his arm how solid the hit is, blood going immediately dark and thick down Luke's chest. As Ben pulls back there's a bright and forceful spray. Luke lifts a hand to his chin like he can catch and hold it there. He produces something like a frustrated gurgle and then Maranda's on him, yelling and swinging, and he drops.

Ben takes a few long breaths. He's dizzy, but able to blink it back, at least a little. Maranda's kneeling on Luke, the empty pistol coming down in heavy, methodical blows.

"Mar," he says, but she doesn't stop. Over and over and over.

"Mar!"

She sits back and takes a breath. She spits, wipes her mouth on her sleeve. Her face is freckled in blood. She stares for a long time at Luke, breathing slow and even.

"Are you okay?" he whispers.

She calmly lays the pistol down and stands, moving toward him.

"I'm sorry," he starts, but before he can say anything more she's kissing him. Her mouth opens, and the vague taste of iron disappears around the warm and wet of her tongue on his. Inside, his feet go out from underneath.

After a minute she pulls back and looks at him.

"Is this *you*?" he says.

She nods, quickly, buries her face in the dark of his collar.

He feels broken open, back from the dead.

"Wait," he says, pulling the rabbit from his pocket. "You forgot this."

The sound of her laugh is clear and bright. "You," she says, and kisses him again.

Around them, they hardly notice the carrier rumbling and vibrating until something bends and a heavy metal groan echoes underfoot. Maranda stops and looks around at the walls.

"Guardian," Ben remembers. "Did Guardian make it?"

"I don't...I'm not sure."

She's weirdly calm, but there's something she's not saying.

"What?" he asks. "What is it?"

"It's Gracie," Maranda whispers. "She's here."

"Mar—"

"I know. She's a…she's one of them. I know. But Ben, please. I need to…I need you to trust me."

He looks up and down the stairs. Licks his lips.

There's a blast outside. The carrier tilts. The lights flicker and little pieces of debris strike the hull.

"Which way?" he says.

She holds up a hand and cracks her neck. "Wait."

MARANDA

The ship is turning itself on and off. The world is darkness, then light.

But she's not panicked, not anymore. There's no chaos spraying out her head. She feels different standing in front of Ben, of Luke, in front of herselves.

Ben's changed too. There's steel in his eyes. She's got his blood on her shirt. There are some things you can't fake.

She feels clean, open.

Gracie's here. She felt her. She knows she felt her. Gracie's been close by the whole time.

"Which way?" Ben says, but she can't concentrate. Someone's clamoring under the surface.

Klara says: *There is something I have to do.*

Maranda thinks: Now?

Or never.

We don't have time. Else I'd say yeah.

Only a second. Please.

Maranda nods. Okay, she sighs. Go for it.

At the bottom of the stairs, Luke is upside down, his throat like torn paper. Klara reaches an arm beneath him. She can still smell his cologne, now mixed with earth and blood. This is the last time any part of him will ever touch her.

She leans in, pulls the cigarettes from his pocket.

"I win," Klara whispers.

Maranda's able to come back no problem. Klara doesn't try to hang on. Maranda gives a little internal exertion—a nudge—and voila.

"Okay," she blinks. "Let's go."

Together, they head for the upper halls. It's like running through a funhouse, the ship slowly falling under their feet. Sparks drop like neon rain.

At the first door Ben tries forcing the handle but it won't budge. Behind him, Maranda rattles Louise's keys.

"Look at you," he says, stepping aside. She unlocks it and tosses them his way.

Inside is a huddled boy, trembling like a bird. He keeps trying to cover himself with his spindle arms.

Ben backs out. Maranda follows. It's not until they're three rooms down that she looks back and sees him hesitating at the door.

The next few rooms are empty. The hallways are slowly inclining. Doors on both sides all the way down. At the end water's already seeping in.

"What do we do?"

She's asking *them,* but Ben answers, "I don't know."

The lights flick off and stay off. Everything goes ghostly. The water is a swirling, angry darkness.

Bridge, Guardian says. Calm and clear.

As soon as the lights come on again, she sees a sign on the wall with an arrow pointing to the upper end of the hall, where another sign points left: BRIDGE. She taps Ben on the back and he follows.

Maranda unlocks the door but Ben still has to shoulder it open with his good arm. She can feel Gracie immediately, but then Ben's hand goes to his mouth, and she follows his gaze out the bank of windows.

Smoke lifts from three or four deep gashes in the earth. Anchorage is bleeding. The sky's an otherworldly orange, clouds rifling by at impossible speeds.

"Good God," Ben whispers.

She scans the room. Panic boils in her arms. Leather chairs in front of dead computer monitors. Switchboards, gauges. A panel of radio equipment. Finally, next to a bank of sea-green lockers there's a series of white pipes—and Gracie, handcuffed.

"Thank you," Maranda whispers. A breath runs all through her. She bends down to touch the handcuffs and they clank to the floor.

A fighter jet rips the sky. Gracie burrows against the floor, sobbing.

"Come on, honey," Maranda whispers, but Gracie covers her head and starts rocking.

Maranda looks at Ben. He's licking his lips and watching the hallway.

She tries to make eye contact, but Gracie won't look at her.

Come on, she says inside. *Help me here.*

Another jet screams overhead. She can feel the vibrations even before it happens. Out her peripherals, she can see maybe a third of the explosion through the windows. Sediment, shatters of airborne concrete. The edge of a firecloud's bloom.

The carrier dips. It keeps dropping.

We came all the way here for nothing, she thinks. We're going to die here for nothing.

But inside, Chipmunk is trying to get her attention. She's saying: *Let me talk to her. Let me talk to Gracie.*

"Gracie," Chipmunk says. "It's me. Remember me? Do you remember? It's me, Chipmunk."

It's like Maranda and Chipmunk are both out at the same time. Like she's helping Chipmunk speak.

Chipmunk holds out the Calico rabbit, flattening her palm to display it, and Gracie sniffles, blinking.

"I brought him back for you. Here. He's yours."

Again it's easy. Maranda takes the reins right back.

Gracie's holding the rabbit, biting her lip.

It's you, Maranda thinks. Gracie's another part of you. Just say what needs said.

"You got dealt a shit hand, Gracie, but you're really good."

Her makeup is all smudged to hell. She's too young to look so battered down.

"Things aren't ever going to be the way they should have been. I'm sorry—I can't fix that. I want to, but I can't."

Gracie's crying now, openly, but she's not breaking eye contact.

"But there's still a whole lot you can do."

The girls, Maranda thinks. There must be another two dozen girls still on board.

"There…there are other people we can help."

Gracie's nods, and she's just reaching for Maranda when another, significantly louder explosion rocks the ship. Blackness throws itself across the window. The carrier lurches weightlessly and the handcuffs scrape all the way to the other side of the bridge, then disappear. Startled, Gracie leaps. Maranda opens her arms, and Gracie goes right *into* her—head, shoulders, all.

Maranda turns a circle but knows already she's not going to find her. Inside, she can feel that something's been set right. Peace rivers her limbs.

She stands, chews her tongue. There are tears all down her face.

"Okay," she says to Ben. "Okay, let's go."

The walls tip deliriously. When the ship falls further, water pulls back into the walls and they have to squish-run the rest of the way up the carpeted junction.

"This way," Ben says, pulling her hand, but she doesn't follow.

"What about everybody else?"

Ben starts to say something but stops. He nods, hesitantly.

She takes them left, running hand in hand. Lights pulse, then go out and stay out. There's a *hum* as the emergency ones come on, illuminating three guards already almost on top of them.

All right Axel, Maranda thinks. *Your turn.*

BEN

It only takes a second. Axel's out for just long enough to elbow the first guy and throw the other headfirst into a wall. He glares the third guy off and stomps a neck, taking a long, slow inhale, like he smells something delicious. Ben barely has time to react before Axel's cracking his neck, switching out again.

It's smooth. Smoother than Ben's ever seen. He's still staring, mouth open, when Maranda comes back. She motions and they keep going.

Deeper in, there's inches of water on the floor, steadily rising. They go in a splashy run, soaked to the shin. Sparks downpour from the ceiling.

He's not thinking, which is welcome. He's still goddamn exhausted and his clothes are heavy with blood and it's hard to move one arm, but things are coming orderly to him, one thought at a time. He runs. He breathes. He feels new. Feels for maybe the first time that he is swimming with the current, that each action has been laid out for him to take up and perform. No second-guessing, no time for doubt.

There's a pounding coming from inside the first door. Ben fumbles through Louise's keys. Outside, the high scream of another jet approaches and departs.

"Come on, come on," Maranda urges.

The door finally swings wide, and two girls charge out, knocking him backward as they slosh up the hall. They have to lurch each leg out to the side to move.

In the next room, there's a girl sitting on the edge of a bed. She doesn't even look up, just watches the water as it swirls her legs with nothing more than the mildest curiosity. Her jeans are wet up to the crotch. Maranda goes in, shakes her by the shoulder, but the girl only blinks.

"Come on," Maranda says. "You need to get out of here."

Finally, the girl comes to, cracking out her neck. A familiar motion to Ben, now.

In places, the water's risen about to his thighs. The last few doors are hell to open. He's got to put all his weight to it. In the final one there's a woman on her bed with hands braced against the ceiling. An end table floats from one side of the room to the other, the lamp still upright on its surface. As soon as they get the door open the woman executes a graceful dive and paddles for the stairs.

Outside, there's a series of percussive strikes. Maranda has to yell at him over the noise.

"Ben, that's it. Let's go!"

She pushes off, propels herself doorjamb to doorjamb, then up out of the water. He's never seen her like this, so muscled, determined. So ready for anything.

He turns to check the hallway one last time. The doors are all open. Everything is dark. You can hear metal straining against itself. There are screams outside, a few jets, and then something far off but impossibly, ungodly loud. He feels the noise constrict and release his heart. Things slow. The ship lurches, and all the water in the hallway buckles and races toward him, but still he has the feeling that each step is laid out, waiting. He takes a breath and dives, all the way to the bottom, where everything is quiet and slow. A weighted wave rolls right overtop him.

When he breaks the surface again he's up against the ceiling. Nothing is making any noise at all. Maranda is on the stairs, waiting.

Okay, he thinks. It's time. He swims toward her. Follows her up the stairs and out.

MARANDA

She pauses at the hatch and takes a breath. What's coming can't be any worse than what's behind, but the sight of it still makes her gasp.

The deck's canted to a crazy angle. Orange water pools over the stern, surging like it's midway through consuming that end of the ship. Half of the MAYA III has settled to the port floor—the other half is airborne and dripping.

She takes a few slow steps. It's impossible to tell if it's day or night. The sky is bleeding fire, scudded with mountains of smoke that move rapidly in several different directions. There's a circle of light, a fantastic eye that she honestly can't tell is the sun or the moon or something else entirely.

Most of the buildings are gone. There's smoke and dust thick in the air, smaller fires burning in the distance. Above them is a cluster of purpled clouds in the vague shape of a fist, hanging so perfectly it looks projected from the city's center.

Ben notices it too. She watches him stare at it for a long time and then, finally, nod. As if things could be no other way. Gently, she puts her hand in his, and they make their way down.

A few people stumble the streets, coated in white. Most of the girls from the ship have run off, but one is just sitting with her legs splayed, scratching at the ground. She's covered in so much ash you can't tell the color of her hair.

Maranda stoops and begins to clear away the girl's eyes. The girl jumps reflexively, but then reciprocates, wiping a small smudge from Maranda's cheek.

"Thank you," Maranda nods.

As they walk, she feels a few of the girls following behind. Weirdly, she's not worried at all. It's like fear has been flushed down the center of her. Everything is quiet. You can hear things clicking, releasing. Can almost hear the Earth grinding on its way.

Ben walks ahead. He pauses at an intersection and looks into the sky. There's something solid and sure on his face. It's not fear, she realizes, he's not looking for planes. It's hope, and even though she's got no idea for what, she feels it too.

He tips his head down the first road. "That way?"

To the left are dead traffic lights, cars upside down or on their sides, wheels still spinning. The other way—more of the same.

Inside, she feels all her people waiting on her, gathered for her decision. She can almost see each of their faces— Guardian, Klara, Axel, Chipmunk, even Gracie and Hagar and the others. Not quite, but almost.

Bring it, they say.

She nods at Ben, and they step into the road together.

If you or someone you know is in crisis, the National Suicide Prevention Lifeline provides free and confidential support 24/7 at 1-800-273-8255.

Approximately 25 million people are trafficked worldwide. If you or someone you know might be a victim of human trafficking, call the National Human Trafficking Hotline at 1-888-373-7888.

ACKNOWLEDGEMENTS

No book is written alone. *When Fire Splits the Sky* was dramatically improved through the creative efforts of many, many people.

Thanks to Summer Stewart and the entire team at Unsolicited Press for their hard work and belief in this project.

My classmates and instructors at the University of British Columbia were instrumental in this book, particularly Sara Graefe and her Screenwriting class, where this idea first took shape under the title *Consuming Fire*. Cara Violini, Jean Sheppard, Mason Hanrahan, Polina Phokeev, Georgina Beaty, Jordan Peters, Cindy Pereira, Janette Rosebrook, Emily Murray, Todd Light, and Andy Bethune all sharpened the core structure of this story. Thanks also to Timothy Taylor and his Fiction class for their wise feedback and advice as I sought to find ways to capture Ben, Maranda, and the alters in syntactically meaningful prose. Elaine van der Geld, Claire Arnett, Nicola Winstanley, Alyx Dellamonica, Natalie Southworth, Tobin Stokes, Owen Schaefer, Natalie Southworth, Carrie Jenkins, Jordan Peters (again), and Todd Light (also for a second time) all helped enormously in this regard.

A deep thank you to Maureen Medved for enthusiasm and advice through multiple drafts and large-scale structural changes, as well as for perhaps the best writing instruction I have ever received. Thanks also to Sheryda Warrener for careful reading and insight, and to Jason Emde and Owen

Schaefer for reading early drafts in their entirety and offering above and beyond editorial feedback.

Thanks also to: Robert Rosenberg, for coffee and conversation and reading an advanced draft, Laura Davis and Sam Ruck for doing the same, Jake Rothman for providing eyes on a key excerpt, and all of my students, past and present—the things teachers say about finding inspiration and joy in the classroom are cliché but also true.

Thank you to my parents, for years and years of library trips and book-buying.

Thanks to E—for everything.

I benefited enormously from a number of resources on human trafficking, PTSD, addiction, and dissociative identity disorder—too many to list here. Thank you to all of the wonderful people out there fighting to destigmatize mental illness and to support the marginalized and vulnerable.

Thanks to my kids, simply for being yourselves—wonderful, incredible human beings. You've made life as a parent indescribably *fun*.

And, of course, most of all, thanks to my wife, Cat, for love, for everything. From talking through story and motivation for hour upon hour to helping to untangle the most confused plot threads, your heart and mind are all over the writing of this. Furthermore, your seemingly bottomless patience, joy, and tireless love have forever transformed the trajectory of my life. While everyone above has helped this book along its journey, it frankly would not exist without you.

About the Author

Tyler James Russell is the author of *To Drown a Man* (2020), a poetry collection, also from Unsolicited Press. He lives in Pennsylvania with his wife Cat and their children. His other work has been nominated for the Best of the Net and Rhysling Awards, and has appeared or is forthcoming in *F(r)iction, Janus Literary, NonBinary Review,* and *The Sepia,* among others. *When Fire Splits the Sky* is his first novel.

TylerJamesRussell.com
Twitter: @TJamesRussell

About the Press

Unsolicited Press is rebellious much like the city it calls home: Portland, Oregon. Founded in 2012, the press supports emerging and award-winning writers by publishing a variety of literary and experimental books of poetry, creative nonfiction, fiction, and everything in between.

Learn more at unsolicitedpress.com.

Find us on twitter and Instagram: @unsolicitedp

www.ingramcontent.com/pod-product-compliance
Lightning Source LLC
Chambersburg PA
CBHW050828190726
48286CB00007B/2011